TEXAS FRIDAYS

EL PASO

SAM MOUSSAVI

EPIC
Press

El Paso
Texas Fridays

Written by Sam Moussavi

Copyright © 2017 by Abdo Consulting Group, Inc.

Published by EPIC Press™
PO Box 398166
Minneapolis, MN 55439

Cover design by Kali Yeado
Images for cover art obtained from iStockPhoto.com
Edited by Gil Conrad

LIBRARY OF CONGRESS CATALOGING-IN-PUBLICATION DATA

Names: Moussavi, Sam, author.
Title: El Paso / by Sam Moussavi.
Description: Minneapolis, MN : EPIC Press, 2017. | Series: Texas Fridays
Summary: Armando Salguera is a tight end, aiming to make his NFL dream come true. At
    first, things are fantastic during his junior season, but then a position change and a family
    situation from his past threaten to destroy his dreams of a career in football.
Identifiers: LCCN 2016946210 | ISBN 9781680764932 (lib. bdg.) |
    ISBN 9781680765496 (ebook)
Subjects: LCSH: High school—Fiction. | Football—Fiction. | Football players— Fiction. |
    Family problems—Fiction. | Life change events—Fiction. | Young adult fiction.
Classification: DDC [Fic]—dc23
LC record available at http://lccn.loc.gov/2016946210

EPIC
Press

EPICPRESS.COM

For those eager to take liberties with the imagination and stay awhile.
—Pete Simonelli

1

ARMANDO ALWAYS FELT AFRAID THAT HIS FATE would be like that of so many cousins, uncles and more extended members of the Salguera family. He didn't want to bust concrete or clip hedges after finishing high school like most of them had done before him. Armando had a grand dream, a secret one. He was going places.

. . . .

Armando clutched his cup of soda as he waited for his usual order of six tacos. The short cook behind the range sprinkled bits of onion and cilantro on top of the sizzling *carne asada*. All the tacos needed now was a squeeze of lime.

"Fifty-three, order up!" yelled out the mustachioed cook.

Armando stood up and showed the other patrons of the taqueria his entire six-foot-five frame.

"Here you go, Armando," the cook said with a smile. "I hear you gonna do some big things on the field this year."

"I plan to."

He took the platter, sat back down, and proceeded to down each taco in two bites. Six were nothing for Armando. The key was not to eat *too* much. He had a workout to get to. If he wanted to capture his dream, there was no such thing as a wasted day.

"*Gracias*," Armando said to the cook.

He left his favorite taqueria in El Paso and went home to change. As he drove through the only streets he'd ever known, Armando didn't feel any apprehension at the prospect of leaving them in the future.

He knew El Paso would always be there if he needed it. What urged him on was the fact that he didn't know anything about what was beyond those streets.

. . . .

"Hi *mijo*," said Armando's mother, Connie, an emergency room nurse with plump features and a warm smile.

"Hi Mom," Armando said, bending down to give her a kiss on the forehead. She had that tired look that seemed to have been superimposed onto her face for as long as Armando could remember. Yet another reason why Armando *had* to make his dream come true. His mother deserved to be able to stop working so hard.

"How are you?" she asked.

"I'm fine. I just had some tacos over at Gabriel's. Gonna get a workout in."

She smiled as brightly as her tired eyes allowed. Though exhausted all the time, she was proud of her only child's drive to make something of himself. Armando had taken after her in the work-ethic department.

"Isn't tomorrow the first practice?" she inquired. Don't you want to take a day off before the season starts?"

"No such thing as a day off, Mom," Armando said, as he gave her another kiss on the forehead.

He went to his room and changed into his workout gear. He was to meet his favorite cousin, Raul, for a workout in the midday sun. Armando got back into his car and turned on the radio. The dial was tuned to the local sports station, and by chance, the high school sports segment was just beginning.

"I think this is the year for the El Dorado Aztecs," the radio announcer said. "I really do. They have a strong defense with nine returning starters from last year. They have a veteran quarterback in Freddie Sendejo. And let's not forget the running game."

"I agree, Bob—" said the other announcer before Armando spun the dial into the off position.

It burned that he wasn't mentioned as one of the key members of El Dorado's team. But really, why would he be mentioned? He hadn't produced much the season before as a sophomore. He'd caught just twenty passes with only one TD. Armando spent a lot of time dwelling on his wasted sophomore campaign and came to the conclusion that no one could stop him from ascending if he put the work in. Only he could stop himself. Not his coaches. Not his quarterback.

This season was going to be different. This was the year that Armando would make an impact on El Dorado's squad. Opposing teams would have no choice but to account for him. They hadn't seen a tight end his size run like that. Ever. The two inches he'd grown and the fifteen pounds of pure muscle he'd added over the summer were going to be his edge.

Raul leaned on the hood of his car as he waited for Armando's arrival at the park. When Armando pulled up and got out of his car, Raul couldn't help but marvel at his younger cousin's physical stature.

It was not long ago that Raul had been regularly called upon to protect Armando out on the *calles*. How things had changed. His younger cousin could take care of himself now—and everyone else in the family for that matter. Any beefs from the past were now squashed with expediency, for fear of tangling with Armando.

"I still can't believe how you've grown in just one summer, *cabron*," Raul said.

They shook hands and hugged.

"You look good, too," Armando said.

"You're not the only one hitting the weights," Raul said. "I can't look like a sissy out here standing next to you."

"Ready to work?"

"Yeah, let's do it."

They started with some laps around the park to get the blood flowing. Armando ran with ease, while Raul struggled. Raul was not out of shape, he just smoked too much pot. Growing up, Raul's love of smoking weed was one of the few things that Armando did not emulate.

Raul coughed and lagged behind. Armando smiled and looked back.

"You gotta lay off that *mota, carnal*," he said.

"I'm good," Raul said, sprinting to catch up.

When they finished their laps, Raul needed a minute to catch his breath. But Armando didn't waste any time. He did sets of crunches and sit-ups as his cousin coughed up phlegm on the sidelines. Armando's washboard abs flexed with each crunch, and it didn't take long for the girls jogging around the park to notice him. One of them, a short and stacked little brunette, eyed him outright and wasn't the least bit afraid to let her gaze linger. Armando glanced back, but quickly looked away. He liked the attention, but wasn't ready to act on the temptation, for fear of his girlfriend, Anna, slicing his throat if she even caught wind of him so much as looking at another girl.

"You see the *tetas* on her?" Raul said with a cough,

still out of breath. "They were bouncing up and hitting her in the face as she jogged."

"Yeah," Armando said, launching into another round of crunches.

"Now that you're all jacked . . . " Raul said.

Armando finished his set, sat up, and eyed his cousin. He was going to say something, but Raul saw the look and said it for him.

"Anna," Raul said, rolling his eyes.

"How do you know that Anna isn't the one, the girl I'm going to marry?"

Raul ignored his younger cousin's plea to lay off him. "Listen, she's gotta understand that you're coming up, and that there are bound to be other girls," Raul said. "If I were you, I'd just tell her that."

The sheer repetition in Raul's sentiments had almost swayed Armando before. But instead of allowing Raul's words to seep in and have a real impact, Armando would think about kissing Anna for the first time when they were in the sixth grade. He thought about the first time they had sex—sloppy, messy, catastrophic, funny, as he and Anna looked back on it now. Anna was the only girl Armando had ever known. She was loyal and had known Armando before football was ever a thing for him. She didn't love him because he was a football player, and Armando liked that.

"Whatever," Armando said as he got to his feet. "Stop talking. I gotta work."

The two cousins started with drills meant to build stamina and agility. Raul played the part of a linebacker who threw all of his effort into jamming Armando off the line of scrimmage. As a tight end, Armando rarely received the privilege of a free release off the line. El Dorado wasn't falling in line with the current high school trend of splitting the tight end out as a part of the spread offense. His offensive coaches favored a pro-style attack—old school offense with a tight end that blocked *and* caught passes. This style of offense featured an in-line tight end and a fullback. All told, Armando would have to be able to beat jams off the line.

After Raul gave a half-hearted effort during a rep, Armando stood chest-to-chest with Raul

"Hit me harder. I mean, really hit me. Try to lay me out," Armando said.

"I'll try."

"Try harder," Armando shot back, and then smiled. "Stop being a little *puta*." Armando knew what he was doing. He knew there was nothing like the magic p-word to get what he needed out of his cousin, Raul.

"Hey," Raul said with fury in his eyes. "I ain't a bitch."

Armando eyed him back. "Well, prove it," he said.

The cousins got into their stances again: Armando in a three-point stance, and Raul in a two-point. Armando barked out, "Hike!" And this time, Raul jabbed his younger cousin off the line as hard as he could. The blow jolted Armando, and the ferocity of it was exactly what he was looking for. He needed to get better with each and every rep he took. After taking the violent jam and getting up-field for his route, Armando chuckled to himself. At the end of the day, he could always rely on his older cousin.

They continued with the drill for the next ten minutes before switching to routes on air. As a soccer player, Raul didn't know the first thing about playing quarterback. But in a pinch, he was an adequate passer. They started with simple five-yard routes, either breaking in or out. Raul again marveled at his cousin's fluid ability to move, despite his size.

Next, Armando ran a series of "seam" routes from both sides of the line of scrimmage. The seam route was Armando's favorite. He loved the danger involved. There was something about running across the middle of the field and pulling down a catch in traffic. The fact that he could have his head taken off by a safety actually excited him.

"Alright," Raul said. "My arm is tired."

"You're tired?"

"Yeah! And don't you have practice tomorrow? Don't you want to be fresh?"

"No off days."

Another girl, this time a blonde with long legs and a flat stomach, jogged by. Her midriff was exposed and flexed with each upward thrust of her legs. Armando's eyes followed until she ran out of sight.

"You better have that talk with Anna," Raul said.

"Man, shut up. You know I don't care about any of that stuff," Armando said, only half-believing his own words. He had never been in the spotlight before. He didn't really *know* how he would react. One thing he promised himself was that when his time to shine did come, he'd try his hardest not to give in to temptation.

The two cousins walked over to the edge of the park near their cars and sat down underneath the same tree they'd sat under when they were kids.

"Can I tell you something?"

"Let me guess," Raul said.

"Okay."

"You're thinking of messin' around on Anna?"

"No! Idiot. Is sex all you think about?"

"Pretty much," Raul said with a smile. "I mean,

it's not all I think about, just a lot of what I think about."

"You're the only person I've ever told this to."

"You haven't told me yet."

"You know what I mean."

"What is it?"

"I have this dream." Armando said, looking his cousin right in the eye. "No, it used to be a dream. But now it feels real. Like I can reach out and touch it."

Raul saw the seriousness in his younger cousin's eyes. He knew when to take Armando seriously. Raul had seen Armando grow up to be a person that the Mexican community in El Paso looked up to. Armando's next step would be for the *gringos* to start taking notice too.

"*Dimelo*," Raul said.

"I'm gonna go all the way to the NFL," Armando said, and the words sounded so sweet coming out of his mouth that he repeated them in his head.

"Like Tony?" Raul asked rhetorically.

"Like Tony."

"I think you can do it, *carnal*," Raul said, looking into his cousin's eyes.

"You do?"

"I think you're gonna get out there this season and do your thing. And all these colleges are gonna be drooling all over you."

Armando remembered growing up with Raul and how his older cousin had protected him from the neighborhood kids before he knew how to protect himself. Armando was thankful to have a *primo* like Raul in his life.

The two cousins stood up, and the bigger one gave the smaller one a hug.

2

Tony Gonzalez was Armando's role model. The long-time NFL tight end who played for the Kansas City Chiefs and Atlanta Falcons, breaking every important league record for tight ends along the way, was also a Mexican-American. That meant the world to Armando. Tony Gonzalez looked and sounded just like him.

So it was no surprise that Armando woke up early the next morning and stared at the poster of Tony G. on his wall. The first practice of the season was only two hours away and Armando could hardly wait. He was ready to show how all his hard work over the summer had paid off. And he needed to do it *now*. This year, his junior year, was paramount for him if he hoped to secure a college scholarship. He wanted the scouts to see him shine from the very start of the season to the end of it. His goal was to have a Division I scholarship locked up by season's end. The first stop on his NFL dream.

. . . .

The late summer sun seared above El Dorado's practice field, and it wasn't even eight o'clock in the morning. Armando arrived at school an hour before any of his other teammates and, out of habit, went out onto the field to get a sweat. The first to join him was the team's starting quarterback, Freddie. They started by tossing the ball back and forth before moving on to routes on air.

"Damn, you're fast," Freddie said after a deep completion down the seam. "You weren't this fast last season. You weren't even this fast during passing league in the spring."

"I hit it hard this summer."

"Bulked up too. You're huge, man."

Armando nodded, and as he did, his right bicep flexed involuntarily. "When you're in trouble this season, look to me. You can depend on me."

Freddie sensed the earnestness in Armando's brown eyes; they were almost too intense to look at. Especially that early in the morning.

The rest of the team joined them in small bunches, and a little after that, the coaches came. El Dorado's head coach was a man by the name of Len Committee. He was a Texas High School football lifer, meaning that this was not his first rodeo. Committee focused on the defensive side of the ball, leaving the offense in the hands of his assistant head coach and offensive coordinator, Mike Clark. Clark liked to pound the ball in the running game. It would be Armando's job to show Clark that throwing the ball to the tight end would prove to be a viable option to go along with El Dorado's vaunted running attack.

As the team stretched, Committee and Clark stood side by side, arms crossed.

"You see Salguera?" Clark asked. "Must've put on ten, fifteen pounds of muscle over the summer."

Committee nodded.

"The kid's packed and still runs like a gazelle," Clark added. "Freddie was raving about him to me before the team started stretching."

Committee didn't react. He had been at this too long to be swayed by off-season conditioning work. Committee needed to see a player improve *on* the field. "Let's see how he does out here," he said.

"Was Salguera in our weight room this summer? I didn't see him once."

"Uh uh," Committee said, "he worked with his own trainer."

It was Clark's turn to nod, and Committee blew his whistle to start the first official practice of El Dorado's season.

Armando started out practice with the offensive lineman because tight ends were looked upon first as blockers in El Dorado's outfit. Clark liked the fact that Armando could run fast, but his devotion to the power game meant that players had to be able to block if they wanted to see the field.

The blocking drills were easy for Armando. He blew any and all comers off the ball during one-on-one drills. It didn't matter who lined up in front of him: defensive linemen, seven techniques, rush linebackers. During one memorable rep, Armando drove a sophomore defensive end all the way into the woods at the edge of El Dorado's practice field. He helped the sophomore up and out of the shrubbery before patting him on the helmet. The sophomore stared in awe at Armando as the two of them made their way out of the woods and back onto the field.

The next part of practice would be an opportunity to shine for Armando—the seven-on-seven drill. Here, he could show off his speed, as well as the hands to go along with it. On the first snap of seven-on-seven, Armando ran a flare route into the left flat, and Freddie hit him in stride. Armando caught the ball cleanly and turned upfield. With the drill being a non-contact one, a pursuing defensive back tried to take an angle to "tag" Armando down. But his burst was too much, and Armando gobbled up the green grass between himself and the safety, before streaking down the sideline and into the end zone untouched.

That first play of the drill got Clark's attention. He sent in the next play to Freddie via hand signal. It was a route combination that sent Armando into the middle of the field where all of the traffic would be. Clark was trying to figure out if Armando could catch a pass in the midst of chaos, something Armando had struggled with the season before. Freddie took the simulated snap and dropped five steps. His first read, a curl to the left, was covered. He then snapped his head around and saw his big tight end flash open. When Armando showed his hands, Freddie released the pass. At this moment, there was heavy congestion in the middle of the field. Hector Dominguez, El Dorado's starting middle linebacker with a compact build, had a beat on Armando, as did the team's starting free safety, Monty Mitchell, who was coming down to break up the pass. Armando snagged the pass again with all hands, then eluded Dominguez and bounced off Mitchell after a shoulder-to-shoulder thud. Though it would probably be more accurate to say that Mitchell bounced off of Armando.

Armando ran into the end zone once again. That made two touchdowns on the first two snaps of seven-on-seven. When they retreated to the huddle, his offensive teammates gathered around him with eyes wide and mouths agape. With El Dorado's historically reliable running game and Armando playing like *this*, there'd be no stopping the offense.

On the third rep, Armando came out. Clark inserted another tight end, a sophomore named Carlos Fernandez, into his place. Clark signaled in the next two plays to Freddie so that he'd have the chance to talk to Armando. Armando grabbed a water bottle and took a knee as Clark approached.

"Nice job, Salguera," Clark said.

"Thanks Coach," Armando said before squeezing a stream of water into his open mouth. He then sprayed some water onto his forehead and down the back of his neck, trying hard not to let the triple-digit temperatures whip him. The sun was baking him, but the physical discomfort meant nothing to Armando. He had defeated pain during his off-season workouts and wasn't about to show any weakness in front of his teammates and coaches just because of a little sun.

"You did the right thing on that last play," Clark said. "You split two. Fantastic job."

"I saw the safety coming down out of the corner of my eye. I knew it'd part if I split it."

Clark patted him on the back of the shoulder pads.

Armando stood up and threw the water bottle back to one of the team assistants. "I'm ready to go back in, Coach."

"Okay," Clark said.

Armando strapped on his helmet and re-entered the huddle. Freddie shared the play, and it called for Armando to streak down the middle of the field. This was the route he was waiting for—the seam.

Before breaking the huddle, Freddie looked to Armando. "If he plays you even, I'm gonna put it on your back shoulder."

Armando nodded.

Freddie snapped the ball and took a seven-step drop. The defense dropped into a cover-two shell. Dominguez, the middle linebacker, carried Armando up the seam while Mitchell, the free safety, prowled the deep center of the field. Armando was hemmed in. Freddie sat back in the pocket, a luxury afforded by the non-contact nature of the drill.

"Screw it," Freddie said.

He fired the pass down the seam. Armando's eyes got big as the ball approached with the perfect marriage of arc and velocity. Armando left his feet, and skied over the two defenders. Neither Dominguez nor Mitchell could break up the pass. Armando was too tall and wide to get over or around. The defenders simply hoped the pass was overthrown.

Armando caught the ball at its highest point with one hand. He instinctively tucked the ball into his body before the inevitable three-car collision. Dominguez and Mitchell took the worst of it—as they had for the majority of seven-on-seven—careening into one another instead of Armando. By the time Armando got up off the turf with the ball in his possession, the rest of his offensive teammates had already joined him in the end zone for a celebration. Three plays. Three touchdowns. Freddie was the first one down there to rejoice, sprinting into the end zone and jumping onto Armando's back like the symbolic monkey that sat there during his summer workouts. Each member of El Dorado's offense believed that he was, in fact, witnessing something special.

The defense, on the other hand, was angry at the prospect of being shredded by *one* player. Coming into the season, El Dorado's defense was supposed to be the more relied upon entity, but with Armando playing at this newfound level, perhaps the opposite was true.

. . . .

After seven-on-seven the team took a water break.

"Dude, you are a beast!" Freddie screamed at Armando.

Clark came over. "Talk to you a sec?"

"Sure Coach," Armando replied.

"I just talked to Coach Committee, and both he and I want you to be more of a vocal leader this season."

Armando smiled.

"Because of your dedication to off-season work and the plays you're making out there," Clark said with a nod to the field, "the rest of the guys have taken notice."

"I got you, Ccoach."

"We're gonna start with some power plays at the beginning of the scrimmage here. Show me some of that blocking technique I saw during individuals. Get 'em going out there."

Armando nodded. "Okay."

Committee blew his whistle and it was time for the first scrimmage of the season. The scrimmage would be live, full speed. This was the part of practice that Armando looked forward to. He felt like no one could tackle him—not even a prideful defense, eager to make amends after a shoddy showing earlier in practice. Armando didn't have time to go half-speed anymore. He wanted everyone's best because the way he saw it, that's what the NFL would be like. The best football players on the planet going at each other full speed.

On the first play of the scrimmage, Clark called an off-tackle run to the strong side, Armando's side. This was a staple play in El Dorado's offense, and it was Armando's job to kick out the defender at the edge of the line of scrimmage. This would open the hole for the running back.

Freddie shouted his cadence, and as soon as the

ball was snapped, Armando took a quick step with his right foot and drove the defender, who was lined up on his outside shoulder, off the ball and out of the hole. El Dorado's starting tailback, Howard Martino, sprinted through the hole and gained thirty yards.

"Atta baby, Salguera!" Clark yelled.

The next play called for Armando to shift from his tight-end position to the fullback spot in the backfield before the snap. His job was to serve as lead blocker for Martino. Armando had also worked on becoming more versatile during the summer, studying the shifts and responsibilities within El Dorado's offense.

At the snap, Armando darted through the line of scrimmage between the left guard and center. The first defender he saw was the weak-side linebacker. Armando wedged the defender out of the hole and, when the back was sprung, showed off his speed. He sprinted and not only caught up to Martino but also made the block that escorted the ball carrier into the end zone.

Clark and Committee stared at each other in disbelief.

"Boy is he getting it done," Len said, his version of effusive praise.

"That was one of the most incredible displays of athleticism I've ever seen," Clark raved.

"Uh huh."

"Salguera's unstoppable as a pass-catcher, but I just hate to take him away from blocking," Clark said, the wheels in his mind already churning. "He might be an even better blocker than receiver."

"Scary," Committee added.

Committee didn't offer guidance or suggestion. The offense was Clark's. Committee didn't put his nose into it, and both he and Clark liked it that way. But this situation with Armando was a dilemma. Clark was a staunch believer in the power-running game. Armando would be a huge part of that attack with his blocking skills—his combination of strength and football acumen a rarity at the high school level.

At the same time, Clark wanted to exploit

Armando's unique skills as a receiver. This was a true dilemma. Clark chewed on his bottom lip and mulled it over. He eyed Armando and couldn't help but stare at his starting tight end's imposing and rock-solid frame. With Armando spearheading the running game, opposing defenses would be in trouble.

"I gotta make a commitment here," Clark offered without prompting from Committee. His tone lent itself more to contemplation than discourse. "A decision, and then a commitment, really."

"Well reason her out and then make one," Committee said before ghosting onto the field. That was about as much advice as Committee had to offer.

Once again, upon returning to the huddle, Armando was congratulated by the entire offense after making a big play. Freddie gave him a punch to the chest. The next call was for all eligible receivers to run seam routes. The whole key here was for the quarterback to recognize which one of his receivers had one-on-one coverage. Freddie had already made his mind up about this play. He would throw it to Armando no matter what the coverage dictated. Armando had earned this kind of trust. Freddie believed that Armando could come down with the catch, regardless of who was covering him,

A new middle linebacker had been put into the scrimmage—a backup named Remmy Hollins. Armando licked his chops as he got down into a three-point stance and waited for Freddie to snap the ball. Hollins was a hotshot sophomore, and El Dorado's coaches were excited about him. Hollins had flashed during spring work, exhibiting an impressive albeit raw ability to make plays. Rising star or not, Hollins had no idea how much confidence Armando was playing with.

"Poor kid," Armando said to himself, referring to Hollins.

Freddie snapped the ball, and the offensive line created a nice, safe pocket for him to step up into. He eyed Armando the entire time. Though there was safety help over the top, Freddie released the pass in Armando's direction—just as he had intended.

Armando peeked back to the line of scrimmage for a split second before continuing on his route down the middle of the field. He was bracketed by two defenders—Hollins and Mitchell—but knew that he could go up and get the ball if Freddie put enough air under it. The ball did have enough air underneath it, and as it came Armando's way, he left his feet. Mitchell hit Armando early, but the contact didn't affect his ability to elevate. A late defender surged into the play, but Armando kept his eye on the ball and brought it down between the three defenders. Yet that wasn't even the most impressive part of the play. With feline-like agility, Armando stuck the two-foot landing at the back of the end zone, managing to keep himself in bounds while defenders collapsed at his feet.

3

FREDDIE WAS WAITING AT ARMANDO'S LOCKER when the tight end returned from the showers.

"What did you do this summer?" Freddie asked. "I didn't see you here in the weight room one time. Did you come in at night or something?"

Armando smiled as he sat down on a bench. "I worked with a personal trainer," Armando said. "Mad Dog McCree. He's worked with NFL and college players."

"Yeah, I've heard of Mad Dog," Freddie said sarcastically. "How could you afford to work with him? I heard it's like five hundred bucks per hour or something."

"I couldn't afford it," Armando said. "I worked my payments off. And I agreed to pay him back after I make it to the league."

"And Mad Dog went for that?"

Freddie was so fixated on Armando's summer work with the famous trainer that he had missed his tight end's not so subtle NFL proclamation.

"Yeah," Armando said.

"Well it makes sense now. Your improvement, I mean. You got jacked *and* worked out with fools who are gonna be playing on Sundays this fall. The dudes we're playing against aren't gonna know what hit 'em."

Armando nodded as he and Freddie shook hands.

"I can't believe you worked with Mad Dog," Freddie repeated. He walked away shaking his head.

Armando turned to face his locker, closed his eyes, and took a deep breath. All the hard work was well worth it. He recalled the morning early in the summer when he approached the popular trainer, William "Mad Dog" McCree, inside his gym in downtown El Paso. McCree was known all over the country for whipping prospects into NFL shape, yet the trainer's heart and allegiance had always been with those who hailed from El Paso, McCree's hometown. Armando showed up at McCree's gym that morning without invitation or the promise of a hefty payment. Nonetheless, McCree was impressed by Armando's mature vision for his future, as well as by his physical skill set. He also regarded Armando's willingness to work off payment as self-confidence of the highest order.

Sticking to his provincial guns, McCree agreed to start training Armando every morning at six, in exchange for a full day's shift at the gym, plus payment in full if and when Armando made it to the NFL. There were no contracts—just firm handshakes from two El Paso boys.

Armando jumped at the offer, and out of ninety days in the summer, he and Mad Dog worked out together on eighty-five of them. When McCree tried to offer Armando a shift off at the gym, Armando would not accept. He refused any handouts and did not want to leave any portion of his debt unpaid.

Anna wasn't too happy about this summertime arrangement as she barely saw her boyfriend over that time. Anytime over the course of the summer when she did see Armando, mostly for a moment here or there, Anna could see the life in Armando's eyes. He was working for his dream, and she would never dare get in the way of that work.

He credited his work ethic as coming from his mother. His grandmother, though, always credited his father, a man Armando never knew. To him, this man was just a name: Oswaldo Durante. Armando's mother rarely spoke of Oswaldo and why he left to go back to Mexico when Armando was just two years old. The only remnants of kinship between father and son were his *abuela*'s stories.

Abuela lived fifteen minutes away from Armando and his mother's home, and she had been just as shocked as everyone else when her son Oswaldo had vanished fifteen years ago. She didn't believe her son had it in him to leave his wife and child without word. What Abuela focused on instead were the good things passed on from father to son. Things like work ethic. Things that Armando would have to either take or leave. Armando's father was a hard-working man who never backed down from a tough job. That was Abuela's story—and the way she chose to remember her son.

Armando's mother, on the other hand, refused to give credit to a ghost, despite Abuela's view of things. In Connie's eyes, a real man would never abandon his family. Regardless, she never stopped her son from seeing his *abuela* or any member of the ubiquitous Durante tribe in El Paso. Connie never went to those functions for obvious reasons. Armando noticed at a young age that his mother was a good woman, and fair, for allowing him to see his father's family.

Back in the locker room, the rest of the team had cleared out by the time Armando opened his eyes. He went out to the parking lot, gym bag in hand, and hopped into his car. He drove to Gabriel's and had his usual. Anna called while he waited for his order to ask if he had any intention at all of laying eyes on his girlfriend, seeing as they had barely seen one another during the summer. Afraid that she would see her boyfriend even less now that football season had started, Anna conveyed these fears to Armando over the phone. He replied that he'd stop by to see her after Gabriel's, but that he couldn't stay long. He had to get some sleep. The team relied on him now.

. . . .

Anna de la Puente was a tall, thin, raven-haired Chicana, who had spent her entire life in El Paso. In fact, all of her family was from El Paso. You had to go back to her grandfather on her father's side to find the last de la Puente to be born across the border.

She sat on the steps in front of her parent's rancher, her green eyes sad. Armando had fallen in love with those eyes way back in the second grade. Armando parked in front of her house and walked toward his girl. She stood when he got close and then leaned her head on his chest.

"Hi baby," Armando said softly.

Anna didn't respond. She simply nuzzled into his thick arms. She followed that up with another habit she had of smelling the skin on Armando's neck. She breathed in his scent deeply.

"Mmm," she said. "I love your smell right after you take a shower."

They kissed softly.

"How did it go?" she asked.

"It went great."

Although she was happy for him, it was not the answer she wanted to hear. Anna was afraid of losing Armando to football. He was the only guy she'd ever known, and she loved him. Splitting up wasn't scary because of a fear of the unknown for her. It had more to do with the fact that they understood each other. Besides sharing a culture and mother language, they were both determined to get out of El Paso. Anna had a dream too. But athletics weren't her ticket out. Her talent was in the classroom. Anna held a 4.5 GPA while also starring in El Dorado's debate and model UN clubs. She was also known to champion causes all around El Paso, including rights for families that emigrated across the border. Her food and clothing drives for those families were an emphatic source of pride. Anna would no doubt secure an academic scholarship to any university she was accepted to.

"I'm happy for you," she said, hugging him tight.

"I thought about my dad after practice."

Anna's eyes were warmed up with understanding. She had both parents, as well as all four of her grandparents. Yet she understood Armando's pain; the confusing and sometimes maddening feelings brought on by the absence of his father made sense to her, as empathy was one of her many natural gifts.

"What made you think of him?"

"I have no idea," he said. "It was after practice in the locker room. I was sitting at my locker, dead tired, and the thought of my dad just popped into my head."

"I was reading this psychology book yesterday," Anna said.

As Anna started talking about the new book she had started, Armando thought to himself, *Of course you're reading a book about psychology. You're Anna de la Puente, the smartest girl I've ever met. Probably the smartest girl who has ever come out of El Paso.*

"And it spoke about how thoughts can be wishes," she continued. "Like maybe you thinking about your dad is an expression of missing him. Of wanting to see him."

"I don't even know him," Armando shot back. "How could I want to see him?"

"He's still your dad. And it makes sense that on some deeper level, you would want to see him."

"Well, I don't know about that book, Anna. But I do know that I don't miss him," he said. "I don't know him, and I don't want to."

Anna fell silent. Although she never broached the

subject of Armando's father, she was always willing to listen, on the rare occasion when Armando himself mentioned Oswaldo.

"And it doesn't matter anyway. I'm up here and he's down there," Armando concluded.

Anna remained silent. She rubbed Armando's face and looked into his eyes. She leaned in close and wriggled her body up against his. Armando could feel her strong thighs rub against his crotch and could tell what she wanted. He couldn't even remember the last time they had had sex.

"Where?" he asked, with a smile curling onto his face.

She looked at the front door of her house.

"Not here," she said.

"My mom is home tonight," he said. "She worked a double yesterday."

Anna stamped her right foot on the concrete step. That was her move when something was in her way. Always the right one.

She chuckled. "You're turning me into one of the sisters over at Perpetual Adoration."

"I know. I know," he said.

She leaned in and kissed him. She snorted as she put everything into a kiss that was meant to be lead to something much more.

Armando pulled away. He looked over to his car. "We could drive up to the point, do it in the car?"

"Gross."

Armando huffed.

"Okay, well, think, Miss Four-point-oh. Where?"

"Four-point-five."

Armando smiled.

"I don't know," she said. "It's looking like it's not gonna happen."

"I am kind of wiped," he said, a yawn perpetuating itself right after the thought.

"Isn't this something," she said. "Too tired to be with your girlfriend. Too tired even to make love."

Armando didn't say anything.

"Do I have to worry about losing you to some silly game?"

"Now it's a silly game?"

"I don't mean it like that," she said. "I just mean there are more important things in life than a game. Like your girlfriend. Like family. Like you and I continuing our relationship and one day having our own family."

"Anna, we are together," Armando said. "We've been together."

"Yeah, but I hardly see you!"

"I don't need this right now," he said. "Please. You know what is at stake for me right now."

He kissed her on the left side of her neck. His favorite spot to kiss. Then he pulled her close.

"We're always gonna be together. Don't worry."

She believed him, but needed a little something more. Anna needed to feel like she was more important than football. But now was not the time to pressure Armando into that kind of expression.

"Okay," she said. "Go home and sleep. Call me later."

"Okay," he said, kissing her on the cheek again. She turned and gave him one more on the lips.

Anna pulled away and grabbed the knob of the front door. Turning back, she looked at Armando and bit her lip. "Figure out a time and place to, you know, *see* your girlfriend in the next month or so," she said.

"I love you," he said.

"Bye," she said before walking into her house and closing the door behind her.

4

CONNIE WAS IN THE KITCHEN, IN FRONT OF THE stove, when Armando walked into a house that was quiet and clean. It was just his mother and him living there together. Though unusual for a Mexican family to be this small, the scenario worked for Armando and his mother. Connie dated a few men over the years, but never found anyone she deemed worthy to procreate with. She married her work instead. Therefore, Connie's one night off per week was set aside to clean the house and prepare food.

"Hi Mom," Armando said, bending down to give her a kiss on the forehead.

"Hi *mijo*," she replied, pinching Mexican oregano into a sizzling pan.

"Smells good."

"Did you eat?"

"Gabriel's."

Connie frowned, for she knew she had nothing on Gabriel's *carne asada*.

"How was practice?"

"Awesome."

"Hard work paying off?"

"Yeah," he said. "I was unstoppable out there. And the best part about it was that I could feel the rest of the guys looking to me. They didn't say much. I mean, Freddie did. But Freddie just likes to hear himself talk. The rest of the guys, though, they all had this look when I walked into the huddle. I could feel it."

"I'm proud of you, *mijo*. I'll be there for the first game in two Fridays. I took my second shift off that night."

"Thanks Mom."

A moment of silence passed between mother and son as Connie flipped the turkey cutlets she had been sautéing.

"Your *abuela* called. She's having a barbecue tomorrow evening and wanted to see if you could make it."

Armando didn't respond to his mother's prompting.

"It's okay if you want to go."

"I don't want you to be home alone," he said.

"I'm working a double tomorrow," she said. "I picked up a shift for Irene. Her niece is getting christened. If you feel up to it after practice, you should go to your *abuela*'s."

"Okay," he said. "Why is Abuela having a barbecue? Is it someone's birthday?"

"I don't know. She didn't say."

"Maybe I'll take Raul with me," he said.

Connie eyed her son with scorn.

"What?"

"Anyone else you'd like to take to the barbecue?" she asked.

Though Connie wasn't around her son much, she sensed that his relationship with Anna had cooled.

"I'll take Anna too," Armando said, child-like.

"Don't lose your mind on this football thing, Armando," she said. "*And* lose that girl in the process. Anna is a special girl. You don't want her out of your life."

"Football is not a thing, Mom."

"Okay, *mijo*. How *are* things between you and Anna?"

"They're fine."

"I haven't seen her for awhile."

Armando knew the quickest way to end the inquisition was to tell his mother what she wanted to hear.

"I won't mess it up with Anna," he said. "I just saw her and we talked."

"Good."

Connie smiled, and nodded to the kitchen table.

"Go sit. I want you to try this turkey. *Guajolote al Sonora*," she said.

He sniffed deeply and the scent of pan-fried bird brought water into his jowls.

"I know you're hungry again," she said. "Six little tacos don't even make a dent."

Armando smiled. "True."

. . . .

The second practice of the season went much like the first. Armando dominated as both a blocker and pass-catcher. The only principal difference between the two practices was that in the second one, Clark came over to Armando several times to ask which plays he liked and which ones he didn't. This kind of respect was new to Armando. Game-plan input was a select responsibility bestowed on the team's best players. Armando gave his opinions on certain plays and formations, but not without making it clear to Clark that he would not take the responsibility lightly.

After practice, Armando called Anna to invite her

to Abuela's party. Anna accepted and Armando told her to be ready in an hour. He then phoned Raul with the same invitation. Raul said that he would meet Armando and Anna at the party.

Anna and Armando arrived at his Abuela's house. The occasion must have been a noteworthy one because the house was filled with aunts, uncles, cousins, nieces, nephews and friends of the Durante family. Armando received pats on the back and kisses on the cheek from people he knew well, people he knew a little, and people he didn't know at all. He and Anna made their way to the backyard and approached Abuela, who was barking out orders to his cousin Manny, the poor soul whose job it was to man the grill for the occasion.

"Turn that one," Abuela droned, pointing down at a piece of *carne* smothered by charred green onions. "You're gonna burn it, Manny!"

The aroma of the meat wafted through the backyard, causing Armando to sniff at the air like his early predecessors. Anna knew that detached look on his face—the ravenous look that could only be assuaged by grilled meat in large quantities.

"Mmm," he said.

"Easy, tiger," Anna said.

Abuela was a short, stout woman, with a lot of life left in her yet. She continued with the grill commands and eyed Manny with contempt until Armando cleared his throat. Abuela turned, and her eyes widened like silver dollars.

"*Mijo!*" she screamed, hopping over to where Armando and Anna stood. "I'm so glad you came!"

Armando kissed his *abuela*. "Hi Grandma."

Abuela only reached Armando's waist; Anna belly-laughed at the sight of an old woman clutching the lower torso of a hulking young man.

"And you brought your beautiful girlfriend with you. How are you, Anna?"

"How are *you?*" Anna asked, leaning in to give Abuela a kiss on each cheek.

Abuela looked to Armando. "She's such a smart

girl. And gorgeous too. You two will make beautiful babies."

Anna smiled with her eyes at Armando. Armando looked up to the clear blue sky.

"Food smells good," Armando said.

"I'll make you a plate as soon as this *tonto* finishes," Abuela said, slapping Manny on the back of the head.

"Ow!" Manny chafed, rubbing at his scalp.

"In the meantime, go talk to your uncle Gus," Abuela said, nodding across the lawn to Gustavo, Oswaldo's oldest brother. Gustavo, or Gus, as everyone called him, was Armando's favorite uncle. Gus rarely talked to Armando about what his father, Oswaldo, had done. Instead, Gus had made a point of always being there for Armando as he grew. This proclamation was not an empty one either. Gus kept his vow, shuttling Armando to and from football practice—until Armando began driving himself— and spoiling his nephew as much as an uncle could.

"Okay," Armando said. "But tell me something. What is this party for?"

Abuela's eyes lit up and her toothy smile seemed infinite. "That's a surprise, *mijo*. You go talk to Gus and all your cousins first. Then we'll eat. And *then* you'll know what this party is for."

"Okay," Armando said, shrugging to Anna.

Anna broke away from Armando as he walked over to Gus.

"Tio!" Armando called out to Gus's back.

Gus turned around and put his beer down on a small table set up in the corner of the backyard.

"Armando," he said, pulling his nephew in tight for a hug. Gus then craned his neck up to give Armando a kiss on the cheek.

"Jesus!" he said. "Did you grow over the summer?"

"Maybe an inch or two."

"You look like a machine," he said, picking up his beer. "Like the Mexican Terminator or something."

"I put in a lot of work."

"It looks so. Sorry I haven't been around to see you much. Things are busy at work."

Gus owned his own landscape service and was in the process of expanding. Armando knew where his uncle's heart was.

"It's okay, Tio."

"When's the first game?"

"Two Fridays from now."

"I'll be there with the whole family."

"How are Monica and the twins?"

"Good. Monica is inside helping, and the kids are running around here somewhere."

Gus looked up to his nephew with brightness in his eyes.

"What?" Armando asked.

"You *look* like a pro football player," Gus said. "The muscles are everywhere they are supposed to be. Your eyes are serious. You look like you're on some kind of mission."

"I am."

Abuela alerted everyone that the food was ready.

Gus put his arm around Armando as they walked over to the dining tables set up in the center of the yard.

"I see you brought Anna," Gus said.

"Yeah," Armando said. "We haven't been seeing as much of each other as she wants."

"Too wrapped up in your mission, huh?"

"Yeah. She understands. But I'm getting the feeling that her patience is wearing out."

"It'll be okay. You guys have been together a long time. Like a married couple."

Gus chuckled. Armando didn't.

"Hey, Tio," Armando said. "Do you know the reason for this party?"

"No."

Armando looked over to the dining tables, whose collective real estate was quickly being taken up by sizzling platters, steaming pots, and stacks and stacks of pillowy, hand-made tortillas.

"Come on, let's eat," Gus said with a pat on his nephew's broad back. "I know you need a lot of protein to maintain this frame of yours."

Raul joined the party a little after the food was served. The two tables were filled with every kind of grilled meat and vegetable imaginable. There was way too much for the people at the party—even with Armando there—to make a dent. Too much food was part of Abuela's thought process, as she customarily gave out leftovers that would last the week.

After everyone finished eating and the laughter and chatter subsided, it was time for the coffee and cake. You couldn't label it a meal if there wasn't coffee and cake served at its end. The women got up and left the men to digest and continue with their conversations about errant penalty kicks and busting concrete. A few of the women brewed the coffee and served it—black to the adults and with dollops of *dulce de leche* to the youngsters. The cake was Mexican wedding cake, of course, even though as far as Armando could tell, no one was getting married. One aunt cut the cake and another served slices to all the guests. And when everything was served to everybody, the family sat down together and was whole again.

Armando scarfed his cake in two bites and lustfully eyed another slice. Then he quickly thought better of the notion. His workout routine had become religion and so too had his diet. Overdoing it with sweets—"empty calories" as Mad Dog called them— was a no no.

Anna held Armando's hand underneath the table as Abuela made her way to the head of the table.

"Okay," she said.

Everyone had finished their cake. Though they were feeling sleepy from the heavy meal, they tilted their eyes up to the old woman.

"I want to share with you all the reason for this special occasion."

Abuela's eyes started to water, and no one there reacted because it didn't take much to cause her tear ducts to activate.

"I talked to my son a week ago," she said. "I spoke to him for the first time in many, many years."

The backyard was hushed. No one who sat around the table dared to even gasp. The news was startling to most there, and to a few, the revelation was downright disturbing.

Armando's heart sank and his head dipped. Though his eyes hit the ground, he felt the eyes from all around the tables. Anna squeezed his hand tightly.

"Oswaldo is coming back to El Paso soon," Abuela said, wiping the streams that flowed down both sides of her face. "He said he'll be here in the next few days."

. . . .

Armando, Raul and Anna had stayed behind, well after most of the other guests had departed for home. It was dark out and the backyard was illuminated by hanging lights. The festive atmosphere belied the empty feeling in Armando's gut. Beyond that, he was still shocked.

Gus and Monica were still there too, along with their twins. Monica was inside tidying up, while Gus was attending to Abuela in her bedroom. After sharing the news of Oswaldo's plan, Abuela was overcome with emotion and had to be put into bed. She wouldn't stop crying, and that fact stopped Armando from approaching the old woman's room to talk about the bombshell.

Abuela's hysterics aside, Armando couldn't move from the chair in the backyard. He didn't know where to begin to think about this news. Anna was silent, going in and out of the house to help Monica and check on Armando. Raul didn't have much to add because he, too, was floored. Oswaldo's betrayals—the initial one fifteen years earlier and the ongoing one that always hung over his cousin Armando—didn't sting anymore than they would have had Raul been a cousin on the Durante side.

Raul was, in fact, Armando's cousin on his mother's

side, and he too was raised without a father, a commonality that bolstered their bond as they grew older. Raul's circumstances were much different though. His father died in a work accident when Raul was a baby. Still, the two cousins shared the pain of not having fathers in their lives, and that pain was real, regardless of specifics.

Truth was, from the time they hit their teens, Raul was aware of his younger cousin's sensitivity from being betrayed by his father. He knew the time would come when Armando would need to deal with the demons of being tossed aside and then forgotten. Raul just didn't know when that time would come. With the moment finally here, he simply patted Armando on the back.

"I wonder if he wants to see me?" Armando asked.

"I'm sure," Raul said. "That's probably why he is coming up."

"Why? After all these years. Why now? I really don't need this hanging over me *right* now."

Anna came out with solemn eyes. She sat down

next to Armando and rubbed the back of his neck. "You okay, baby?"

"Crazy," he said.

Anna couldn't help herself. She could not stop her brain from going through the permutations of the situation. "Maybe it was your subconscious mind working," she said. "Remember yesterday, when you were thinking about your father? It was your subconscious telling you that he is going to come back into your life."

Raul looked at Anna as if she were a lunatic. Armando rubbed his forehead and then his eyes.

"Not now with this crap, Anna," Armando said.

"What?" she asked. "It could be true."

"Besides," Armando said. "He can't come back into my life because he was never a *part* of it in the first place." He stood up. "He wasn't invited."

"He's still your father," she said.

Armando turned and eyed Anna.

"No, he's not. I hope he's not coming up here to see me because I won't see him."

Anna stood up. "Armando, you need to think about—"

"Stay out of this, Anna."

Armando walked into the house and when he reached the foyer, Gus was exiting Abuela's room. He approached and sighed.

"She's finally down for the night," Gus said.

"Is it true what Abuela said, Tio?"

"I don't know," he said with eyes that turned exhausted in what seemed like a moment's passing. "No one in the family has heard from my brother in more than ten years. Before tonight, I assumed he was dead."

"Why would he come now? After all these years? I don't need anything messing with my head right now."

The shock wore off, and the proximity to Oswaldo's impending arrival spun Armando's mind before throwing it into a frantic loop of questions, none of which could be answered until the ghost from Armando's past returned.

"I don't know," Gus said.

Raul and Anna joined Gus and Armando in the foyer. Anna's eyes were glistening.

"Let me find out what's going on, and I'll let you know," Gus said. "Do you have practice tomorrow?"

"No," Armando said. "Sundays are off."

"I'll come by the house tomorrow," Gus said. "I'll try to see what I can find out from Abuela after she gets some sleep. Until then, keep your mind clear, okay?"

Armando nodded without processing his uncle's request, and walked out of the front door. Anna and Gus exchanged a glance as she passed by. Raul walked out last.

"I'm gonna take you home, Anna," Armando said.

"My parents won't be home until late," she said.

Armando stared at Anna and his eyes were blank. Anna had never seen his eyes without the alertness and acuity that she had come to expect whenever she met his gaze. The way he looked at her over the years—the intensity of the looks themselves—was the thing she longed for most.

"I'm here for you."

"Not tonight."

Anna got into the passenger seat, her mind a blank canvas. If she couldn't rely on Armando's eyes, she didn't know where to rest her hopes in their weakened relationship.

Raul approached Armando. The two cousins looked into each other's eyes, silent, as the warm Texas air coated a full moon over top of their heads.

5

OSWALDO DURANTE DID NOT HAVE LONG TO LIVE. One month. Two tops, if he was lucky. He lit a cigarette in front of the little corner store from which he had bought the pack. Even though it was probably the cigarettes that gave him the cancer, he couldn't stop now. He was dead anyway.

It was hot down in Juarez, Mexico, a dry inferno of static activity until the sun fell. Oswaldo looked out at the road and then further out at the desert. He'd be crossing *that* soon. If lucky, he'd get across to see his boy.

Oswaldo walked along the side of the road and

stopped in front of one of those roadside memorials. Three white crosses stuck out of the hard red dirt. A few candles and a couple of trinkets to help in remembrance of the departed. Oswaldo did not complete the sign of the cross before continuing on his way. A buzzard circled overhead and signaled its presence to Oswaldo. *I'm not dead yet, you bastard,* he thought to himself.

He was to meet a contact that could get him in touch with a coyote—a person, an entrepreneur of sorts, who smuggled people and items across the border and into the United States. Oswaldo needed a coyote to get across because there was no way he could get across legally. His passport was long expired. But that was the least of it. His associates in Juarez, in Sonora, in Mexico City, would never stand for an attempt to get across legally. There was too much heat on him and his associates for that route to be tried. He was fine with getting across this way. With his track set, the only fear was *not* getting across the desert. Oswaldo was in a race with time to see his boy.

When Oswaldo reached the meeting point, a small refreshment stand at the center of Villa San Jose, he stopped and looked for a man from his past. The man he was looking for was not a close friend; he was simply someone Oswaldo knew in passing.

He scanned the faces of the passersby. No one stopped. No one smiled at him or seemed to recognize him. He lit a cigarette and waited patiently. After three minutes, a man dressed in all black approached and stood next to him. They were both silent at first. Oswaldo tried to picture the man's eyes behind the dark sunglasses, but it was a pointless exercise. The man cleared his throat.

"Oswaldo?" he asked in a gruff voice, almost a growl. The man spoke in English. Oswaldo still spoke English himself. Probably with better skill and more nuance than when he was in El Paso all those years ago. Anyone who was anyone in Mexico spoke

English. All of his associates did. And so would the people who'd help him get across.

"Yes," Oswaldo replied.

"Come," the man in black said. "Let's go find some quiet."

Oswaldo followed the man through a tight alley that led to a dead end. There was a time when Oswaldo dressed in all black himself, just like the man he followed. Stylish and solemn, with a pair of black sunglasses to tie it all up. The entire outfit itself was a statement against those who dared to get in the way of his associates, and by extension, Oswaldo himself. But those days were long gone for Oswaldo. He didn't have the time nor the energy to be stylish. He just wanted one day with his son.

At the end of the alley sat a table with two chairs. There were two big, brown-skinned men at the end of the alley, guarding either side. They were looking into the alley, past Oswaldo and the man in black.

"Sit," the man in black said.

Oswaldo sat and at the moment, the pain in his

body was dull. He had learned to manage the discomfort over the years but when the pain went rogue and changed into a sharp awareness—like an ice pick repeatedly plunged into the spine—that's when he knew he was in for it.

He shifted to a position that put the pain into the back of his mind. The man in black sighed lightly as he took a seat.

"Do you remember me?" the man in black asked.

"I need to see your eyes."

The man in black took off his sunglasses. It was then that Oswaldo recognized the face. He couldn't conjure up a name, however. Names were difficult after many years. But in Mexico, oftentimes street names were particulars that did not matter. They were simply markers. In Oswaldo's specific field, a man's name was rarely his given name anyway.

"I know you," Oswaldo said. "I don't have a name, but I know you."

"Funny. I know your name," the man in black said.

"I have nothing to hide anymore."

The man in black leaned back in his chair and looked to the guards on either side of his shoulders. The two men continued staring straight ahead into the alley.

"You've caused a lot of pain," the man in black said.

Oswaldo thought about that. He then thought about his boy. "Yes," he said.

"And now you are in pain, no?"

"Yes."

"And you don't have much time."

"No."

"Why is it you must get to America?"

Oswaldo's eyes lit up with fire. His right hand shook with rage. "They know why. All of them know why."

"Tell me," the man in black said calmly.

Oswaldo hated to be tested. People who tested him generally paid a price. The biggest price. But those days were over now. Oswaldo was a sick man. He just had to get across and see his boy.

"I have to get across," Oswaldo said, "to see my boy."

"The boy you left?"

Oswaldo looked away from the man in black. He couldn't look him in the eye and talk about his son.

"Yes," he said with haste and annoyance in his voice.

"And you are what, 'retired' now?" the man in black asked.

"Yes."

"So you will die in America?"

"That is correct."

"Good. Once you leave this place. You cannot come back."

"*Sí*."

"Okay."

The man in black whistled and the guard on his left snapped to life. The man in black whispered into the animate guard's ear, and then with a nod, both of the guards bombed down the alley.

"They will get you a ride to the desert. You have

to cross a good part of it on foot. The desert must be crossed at night. Can you even do that right now?"

Oswaldo thought of his son. "Yes."

The man in black eyed him uncertainly and shook his head. "They will take you to eat before you cross the desert tonight. Eat as much as you can. For the energy. They will also give you water, but use it wisely. When you get across and get to the meeting place near the border, you'll connect with our coyote, Naranja."

"Naranja?"

"*Si*. You'll understand when you see him," the man in black said with a malignant smile.

The engine of an SUV roared and then chugged behind Oswaldo. He turned to see the black truck with tinted windows at the mouth of the alley.

"Go with them," the man in black said with a nod.

Oswaldo got up from the table and the man in black did the same. He replaced his sunglasses on his head. He put out his hand for Oswaldo to shake. He did.

"Good luck," the man in black said.

Oswaldo nodded and walked back down the alley. The walk down to the black SUV felt like it took forever.

. . . .

The two guards took Oswaldo to the home of a woman, who had a large spread of food prepared. The food was all laid out on the table in her dining room. Two other men were brought to the home by another pair of guards. When it was time to eat, the seven men sat down at the table and passed around the platters filled with meat and vegetables. The woman did not join them. She lingered in the kitchen with an open ear to any requests for more food or something to drink. But there were no such requests. The table was filled with more food than the seven men could possibly eat.

Oswaldo ate very little and said even less. There was little to no conversation around the table in fact.

The only comment coming Oswaldo's way was a reminder to eat as much as possible now in preparation for the unknown of the Juarez desert. Oswaldo forced down as much food as he could, falling way short of the pace set by the other two traveling men.

After dinner, Oswaldo went into the woman's backyard to smoke. She slipped out of the kitchen and joined him. She was middle-aged like him, with a soft face. He offered her a smoke and she accepted. He lit it for her and the two of them exchanged a passing glance that turned into a lingering one.

"You're going to America?" she asked.

Oswaldo was surprised by both the use and quality of her English, but then quickly remembered his business, and that this woman was no doubt tied to it.

"Yes."

"You don't look so good," she said, blowing a stream of smoke into the hazy, thick air.

"I'm not doing so good."

A silence hung. But she couldn't help but ask the next question.

"Then why would you be crossing the desert?"

Normally when Oswaldo was working, he'd lie. Lying had become such a habit for him that he didn't even know which life was real anymore. But he wasn't working anymore. With the little time he had left, he wanted to be honest. And this was a start.

"My boy," he said, "he's up in El Paso. I haven't seen him for fifteen years. The doctor told me I don't have much time."

She opened her mouth but no words came out. She nodded with sympathy in her eyes instead.

Oswaldo looked up into the sky and behind the haze, he saw a full, bright moon.

"It's getting dark," he said. "I think we should start soon."

"*Sí*," she said.

* *

Two of the guards dropped the travelers at a point where there were no houses or life beyond the creatures that slithered and scurried along the desert floor when the sun went down. Each traveler was given a canteen of water as well as a bit of jerky and a few sweets for energy. The guards didn't know exactly how far they needed to walk, though what they did know was that it would take a long time. Before driving off in the SUV, one of the guards informed the travelers as to the approximate meeting spot with Naranja. The guard added that it was no guarantee that they'd reach him. Oswaldo knew that his odds were the lowest.

The air was cool at that time of night. The three travelers started on their way. They heard the black SUV getting farther and farther away behind them. Oswaldo started out up front. There were no words passed between the three men for an hour or so.

A rabbit jumped in and out of their path.

"Watch out for rattlesnakes," one of the men said.

A coyote yipped in the distance.

Oswaldo lit a cigarette and the dull pain returned in his lower back. He thought about how severe the pain would be if he was actually able to cross the desert alive. But he didn't care. He was on a mission.

After another thirty minutes, the two men lagged behind Oswaldo. He heard their boots stop in their tracks and he turned around to them.

Is this it? Oswaldo thought. *Is this my reward for all I've done?*

"Let's take a break," one of the men said.

"My feet are on fire," the second one said.

Oswaldo sighed in relief. These men hadn't been hired to finish the job that the cancer inside of him had started.

"I'm not stopping," Oswaldo said. "You can, but I'm not."

He continued on. The two men looked at each other and quickly caught up. The three walked at a steady pace now. The sounds of their steps on the desert floor coalesced into a rhythmic expression that echoed in the void surrounding them. The creatures that were out at night watched the three travelers in lust. Two were weak and the other was determined to cross no matter what stood in his way. They knew. The march continued, mile after mile. Fatigue could not touch Oswaldo.

The night sky darkened a shade, and Oswaldo took a sip of water from his canteen. He looked back to see the two men struggling to keep pace. He smiled a private smile; cancer possessed his body, not theirs.

The three travelers continued; Oswaldo stayed at a steady rate, setting the pace, while the other two floundered. After another hour or so, Oswaldo finally stopped. The sky was indigo now, telling him that it was around four a.m. He wasn't in any discomfort. His back was fine. His chest wasn't filled up with blood or mucus. He just wanted a smoke. The two men stared at him as he lit up.

He breathed out the first hit with a pleasurable "ah!" For a moment, he had forgotten that he was out in the middle of the desert with two perfect strangers. He closed his eyes and focused on the magnificence of the cigarette burning in his hand. When he opened his eyes and saw the two men, it all came back.

"*Quieres?*" he asked, holding out the pack.

The two men shook their heads.

"Let's go," he said, putting the onus on them, not only to continue but also to keep up with this withering man.

As the sky lightened in gradations, Oswaldo's determination was as strong as ever.

Before the diagnosis, he had not planned on going up to see Armando. The stink of abandoning was still too strong, and fifteen years did nothing to wash it away. The shame of leaving his young wife and two-year-old son was too much to bear. That's why he never called or wrote. That's why the thought of going back to El Paso never even crossed his mind. But the doctor's prognosis changed all of that—stomach cancer that was spreading up to his chest and into his lymphatic system.

After all of the death he, Oswaldo, had caused with his work, death was now staring right back at him. That prognosis was a fire starter. It was either attempt to see Armando now or wait for him up in Heaven. Problem was, Oswaldo wasn't one hundred percent sure there was a Heaven. And if there was, he was pretty sure he wouldn't get an invitation in.

"Hey man," one of the men said from behind.

Oswaldo turned around to face him.

"We need to take a break," he said. "We've been walking for eight hours or something."

The sun was coming up, breaking over a mountain peak in on horizon, putting it around seven a.m.

"We've been walking for ten hours," Oswaldo said.

"Okay, ten," the man said. "Even more reason to stop and take a break."

"I'm not stopping until I reach Naranja." Oswaldo turned back around and continued on his way.

"Are you crazy, man?" the man asked to his back. "You're not gonna take a break?"

"Walk or stop," Oswaldo said without turning around, "it doesn't matter to me."

The sun was high and Oswaldo was all alone. The way he figured, he had about ten to twelve miles left. He had heard that it took a full twenty-four hours of walking to cross the Juarez desert. Maybe a little less at the pace he was going. The other two men were either asleep or dead at the spot he had left them. There was no way their meager food and water supply would last if they weren't moving while consuming small portions of it.

The morning sun threatened to burn a hole inside of all things below. Oswaldo shed his sweat-soaked coat, as it only weighed him down. His back and feet throbbed with precise shots of pain, and he wasn't sure if it was the cancer bearing down on him with a grave warning, or the fact that he had been walking across the desert for twelve hours. Whatever the source, the pain had him at a crossroads. He forged on thinking of his son and the image of the boy he had held in his arms for those first two years.

Even then, Armando was a big boy. Oswaldo wondered what his son looked like now, and if he had kept growing at that rate. Over the course of the fifteen years, Oswaldo had had passing thoughts of sending a gift Armando's way on his birthday or for Christmas. But the thoughts never materialized. It was just easier to forget about Armando. He couldn't live the life he chose if he was constantly thinking about another life he had left faraway. The life he chose down in Mexico needed all of his attention. He would have died if he allowed his mind to stray too far from the present.

In the eyes of his associates, Oswaldo was a hard worker. The hardest worker. If you needed something done, no questions asked, Oswaldo Durante was the choice. What Oswaldo let go of as a father was made up for in spades as a worker.

But now, his present was steeped in the past, and his reputation couldn't help his cause in El Paso.

Oswaldo came to a four-way road in the desert that led to infinity in all directions. He stopped in the middle of the road and steadied himself on a sign that was four arrows with the name of four "ghost" villages painted on them. Who knew if any of those places had even a single inhabitant?

The desert isn't a place to live, he thought. *It's a place to pass through or die.*

A buzzard—a different one from the day before, perhaps—circled over top of his head. It sounded its shrill call and Oswaldo looked up weakly.

"*Chingate*," he said.

His vision was blurred and his head throbbed with intermittent, albeit vicious, cycles of sharp agony. Violence and then reprieve. Violence and then reprieve.

"I deserve this. I know," he whispered to no one. "I just want to see my boy. Don't take me now. Please."

He let go of the sign and staggered on. The sun was wild, blinding, and fierce. His steps were slow.

"Please," he huffed. "Don't take me now."

A dry flurry of needle-sharp coughs forced themselves out of his chest. He wobbled and then his vision flickered. He coughed once more and a gob of red came up. It was his time. He had to pay for what he had done.

This was the end.

He fell to the scorched earth and the dust enveloped him. He coughed a little more and wiped blood from his mouth. He didn't even have the strength to open his eyes and see the place where he would die.

"Please. Don't let the birds eat me," he whispered.

Distant footsteps approached and in a matter of what felt like seconds, the steps neared.

"Hey brother," a voice said. "Are you okay?"

Oswaldo heard the words and they registered. His throat and lips were too parched to make an attempt at speech.

"Brother," the voice said again. "Who are you? *Esta Durante?*"

Oswaldo opened his eyes and perceived the outline of a moving form. The sun was a halo over top of the form's head. He again thought of holding his little boy before the lights went out.

6

SUNDAY WAS CHURCH DAY IN EL PASO. ARMANDO and Connie woke up for the early mass. Connie was fresh off from working a double shift, and Armando hadn't slept much either, consumed as he was with thoughts of his father. On the fifteen-minute drive to the cathedral, Armando didn't speak to his mother. Connie knew her son. Something had happened the night before.

"Everything okay?" Connie asked, as they got out of the car. "You didn't say how it went at your *abuela*'s house last night."

Armando looked at his mother but was careful to

limit the look to a passing glance. He didn't want her eyes locking with his. If that happened, he'd never be able to hide the news.

"I'm fine," he said before looking down at the pavement of the church parking lot.

Connie didn't press. Perhaps the pressure that would undoubtedly come with his newfound prominence within the team had arrived that very morning, she thought. Maybe her son was tired? Connie knew all about pressure. When her husband picked up and left out of the blue, she had the pressure of the world on her shoulders—an infant son that had to be cared for and no husband to help.

Mother and son walked into the cathedral, and the change in light was harsh to their eyes. Armando squinted until they could readjust. He found a couple of seats in a pew toward the back, and they sat. Connie scanned the cathedral and saw someone she knew. She excused herself, and Armando looked up at the ceiling.

The congregation liked to announce that

membership was open to all colors and denominations. But Armando only ever encountered Mexican-American Catholics. People talked in muted Spanish all around him. He focused on the fresco on the ceiling. Armando had looked up at the ceiling during church for as long as he could remember. When he was a young boy and could hardly sit still, his mother used to tell him to look up at the ceiling because it would make the sermon go by faster. He knew now that this was just a ploy by his mother.

Connie returned and saw her son looking up.

"Ready to talk to me?"

"The sermon is about to start," he said, head still tilted skyward.

"How do you know?"

"The voices are quieting down."

Connie looked to the altar at the front of the cathedral and saw Father Marquez licking his lips, readying himself for the service. Armando fixed his gaze on the altar without glancing at his mother.

"Something happened last night," she whispered. "You're not yourself."

Armando closed his eyes and listened to Father Marquez sing the opening hymn.

. . . .

After the service, Armando felt restless—struck with a sudden urge to get his mind off things. He spotted Freddie out in front of the cathedral and walked over to him.

"Freddie," Armando said.

"Armando," he said. "What's up?"

They shook hands.

"Want to go throw some routes?" Armando asked.

"Today?" Freddie said. "On our day off?"

"Yeah."

"It's like a hundred degrees."

The midday sun was working overtime. It was a good thing El Dorado didn't have practice that day.

"I know it's hot," Armando said. "But we could use the extra work."

"You wanna work out right now?" Freddie repeated. "For real?"

Armando could see the indecision in Freddie—the quarterback liked his time off but was also a fierce competitor.

"I was gonna go see my girl," Freddie said.

"Come on, Freddie," Armando said. He looked his quarterback right in the eyes.

Freddie saw something in Armando's eyes that said he needed to be out on the field, and he needed Freddie to be out there with him. Freddie had no idea *why* Armando wanted to go practice in one-hundred-degree weather, on the team's day off, no less. But Freddie didn't ask any more questions.

"Okay," Freddie said. "I gotta go home and change. I'll meet you at school in thirty minutes."

"Cool. Thanks man."

They shook hands again. Armando went to find

his mother. She was standing with an old woman at the foot of the stairs in front the cathedral.

"We gotta go, Mom."

"What's your rush? Say hello to Mrs. Medina."

"*Hola, Señora Medina*," he said to the old woman. The old woman nodded gracefully.

"Don't you want to go eat?" Connie asked.

In El Paso, a long lunch after church was a tradition adhered to with more faith and devotion than the actual sermon itself. Its promise was the only thing that dragged Armando out of bed on Sunday mornings. Armando knew he had to give up the lunch on this Sunday, however. His mother would make him talk, and eventually, extract the news of Oswaldo's return if they sat down together. Before he told his mother anything about his father coming up to El Paso, he needed to talk to his uncle Gus first to see if there was any more information.

"I'm gonna go work out with Freddie," Armando said.

"On your day off?" she wailed. "You'll fry."

"It's okay," he said. "It'll just be for a little while. Freddie and me, we need to build our chemistry."

"Since when do you not want to eat?" she persisted.

"I'm fine, Mom."

She looked at her son with a crooked eye.

"Okay. We're gonna talk tonight, though," she said. "So don't make any plans. I'm gonna make dinner."

"Okay."

"I'm gonna take the car home to change," he said. "Can you get a ride home from the Mercados?"

"Sure," she said.

"Love you, Mom."

Armando leaned down and gave his mother a kiss. She tried to lock eyes with him, but he wouldn't comply. Connie watched him as he made his way to her car. She sensed the nervous energy in her son's posture after church. That, coupled with his silence before church, cemented it for Connie. Something was up. As soon as he pulled out of the parking lot, she withdrew her cell phone and dialed Armando's *abuela*.

. . . .

Armando changed into his workout clothes and downed a protein shake before leaving the house. The heat outside was nothing to fool around with, and Armando knew better than to go exercise without anything in his system. In the car, he called his uncle Gus and asked him to meet at school after his workout with Freddie. Gus agreed, even though he hadn't uncovered any additional information about Oswaldo. Armando didn't care. He needed to talk to someone, and his uncle Gus was one of the few people he trusted.

When Armando parked in the lot behind school, Freddie was already out on the field. He was rehearsing his pass drops when Armando dropped a gallon jug of water and his keys on the sideline. He joined Freddie on the field. They began playing catch.

"This heat," Freddie said. "Man!"

"Thanks again for coming out, Freddie."

"Don't mention it."

"What did your girl say?" Armando asked, before tossing the ball back to Freddie.

"She complained. But I'll see her tonight."

"Mine's the same way."

Armando extended the distance between him and Freddie by ten yards, and they continued. Armando caught each pass with his hands.

"I'm ready!" Freddie called out.

Armando jogged over.

"You've been with your girl for a while now, right?" Armando asked.

"Yeah," he said. "Graciela. Six years."

"Damn! I thought I was the only one!" Armando said. "I've been with Anna for eight."

Freddie smiled.

"Can I ask you something, Freddie?"

"Sure."

"When you became the starter, how did you handle all the girls coming around?"

Freddie smiled again, this time wider.

"I got caught up a few times," he said. "After the last time, Graciela dumped me. It was for real too. She wasn't just trying to send a message or anything like that. She was done with me."

"How'd you two get back together?"

"It took a month of me begging her to take me back. She finally did when she believed that I was serious, I guess. I haven't messed around on her since."

"Will you ever cheat on her again?"

"I'm gonna try my hardest not to."

"Anna is the only girl I've ever been with."

Freddie spun the ball in his hand.

"Everybody is always telling me that I'd be crazy to let her go," Armando said. "But I don't know. I think about other girls at school or the ones I see around town. And I wonder what it would feel like to be with them, you know?"

"I get you," he said. "Believe me I do. You gotta make that call yourself. I mean, Anna's hot. No offense."

Armando smiled to let his quarterback know that the comment was taken in good spirit.

"But I can see that you would want to be with someone else just out of curiosity."

"How was it when you were with those other girls?"

"It was amazing, I'm not gonna lie," Freddie said. "But when Graciela dumped me, I had to decide between her and the other girls."

Freddie stared into space and pondered the past opportunities to be with other girls.

"It's tough. No one's saying it's easy," he continued, as if trying to convince himself rather than Armando. "But I want to be with Graciela for life. She's good for me and my future."

Armando didn't say anything.

. . . .

After the workout, Freddie took off to be with Graciela. Sweat dripped from Armando's forehead and arms as he sat down on the turf to stretch. His uncle Gus would be there soon, and Armando used the spare moment to take his mind off his father's impending arrival and think instead about his pre-workout talk with Freddie. Freddie had already experienced what Armando was about to go through. As a star player, Armando would attract the attention of many girls at school. But Anna was special. She was not only smart but sexy too. She was also Armando's best friend.

Gus approached from the far end of the field.

Armando stood up. "Tio."

"Sunday workout?" Gus asked, with a smile.

They shook hands.

"I had to do something to take my mind off last night."

"I stopped by your *abuela*'s this morning," he said. "She's still very emotional. You know her."

Armando nodded.

"She doesn't know anything else," Gus said with a frown.

"Nothing?"

Gus shook his head.

Armando stayed quiet.

"No one knows why he left all those years ago, Armando. No one approved of it then, and we don't approve of it now."

"I know."

"I just wanted to tell you again," he said. "Your *abuela* was angry at him for many years. Probably until he sent word to her the other day. But she's old and he is her son. Old age softens a person."

There was a moment of silence between uncle and nephew. Sweat glistened on Gus's forehead.

"Can I tell you something, Tio?"

"Of course," Gus said, wiping his forehead with a napkin he had in his pocket.

"I'm going to make it to the NFL."

Gus patted his nephew on the shoulder.

"I'm just afraid that my dad coming back to El Paso after all these years is going to mess that up in some way."

"It's not," he said. "If making it to the NFL is

your dream, you'll make it come true. A man always has his destiny in his owns hands. No one can stop a man from being what he is meant to be."

. . . .

Armando arrived home and his mother was waiting for him at the kitchen table. There were no aromas wafting through the house, no pots or pans bubbling on the stove.

"I thought you were making dinner," he said.

"I talked to your *abuela*."

Armando tried to look incredulous, but it was no use. He sighed.

"Why didn't you tell me what happened last night?"

"I didn't know how," Armando said.

"Do you want to talk about it?"

"Not really. There's nothing to talk about."

"Do you want to see him?"

"No."

"Because if you do, it's fine. I would never stop you from doing so."

"I don't want to see him. I've never wanted to know him because he never wanted to know me. I wish he would just stay in Mexico and leave us alone. I have enough to deal with as it is."

"I couldn't believe it when your *abuela* told me," she said.

"Same here."

"I wonder what the hell he could be thinking," she said. "Why now?"

"Why now?" Armando repeated.

7

OSWALDO RUSTLED HIMSELF AWAKE. HE COULDN'T see at first. There was just black. His lips and throat were as dry as the boneyard that he had just crossed. His first thought was that this was it. He had reached the end. The big sleep.

"Brother?" a voice from in front of him inquired. "You back?"

Oswaldo opened his eyes again and this time, there was sight. He blinked several times for confirmation and then sat up slowly. The room was warm, the air sticking to his skin. He licked his lips and fixed them to speak. Even this modest act required great effort on his part. He chuckled at the cruelty of it all. He had led a life in which he held great power over others—not quite God but, rather, the executioner.

"Where am I?" Oswaldo asked.

The man gut laughed and a whistling emanated from his nose. Oswaldo could tell from the man's voice and pinched breathing that he was a fat man.

"You made it, brother," the voice determined.

"I made it?" Oswaldo asked. "I'm in El Paso?"

"Not quite," the voice said. "You're one step away. But the hard part is over."

The man stood up and opened the blinds in front of a large window. Suddenly the room was bathed in white light and Oswaldo covered his eyes in defense.

"The other two didn't make it," the man said. "Funny. You were older than them by many years, and I've been told you are quite ill."

Oswaldo's eyes adjusted and he was able to see the man. His skin color was orange, explaining the moniker Naranja. And he was correct. Naranja was a fat man.

"Naranja?" Oswaldo asked.

He nodded.

"Did you save me from the desert?"

Naranja smiled to reveal a set of front teeth that were stained a putrid brown-yellow by coffee and cigarettes.

"I wouldn't say I saved you,'" he said. "I did my job."

"How long have I been asleep?"

"A day."

"Where are we?"

"In a motel next to the border," Naranja said. "I wanted you to be awake before we went across. Once we get there, you'll be on your own. You need to be as strong as possible from this point. I can't stay and watch over you. I have to get right back across."

Oswaldo bristled at the thought of needing a babysitter. He caught a glimpse of himself in the motel mirror and what stared back was not an image of someone who struck fear into others.

"When will we leave?" Oswaldo asked.

"As soon as you are ready. Hungry?"

Oswaldo shook his head. He stood up and the room spun. He collapsed back down onto the bed. Naranja waddled over.

"Easy," he said, with the pinched breath returning. "Would you like to stand?"

Oswaldo nodded.

Naranja helped Oswaldo to his feet and steadied him until he was able to balance himself.

"You're tough."

"Is that some kind of joke?" Oswaldo asked, breathless.

"No," he said. "You walked twenty miles across the Juarez desert. Most healthy men could not do that. But you . . . "

Oswaldo didn't need compliments. He had his purpose and that was enough. He wondered then if Naranja knew the reason for his journey.

"You should eat."

"Forget about food," Oswaldo said. "I want a smoke."

Naranja laughed from deep down in his potbelly.

"Okay," he said. "We'll have a smoke and then go. Why don't you at least take a shower first?"

Oswaldo looked into the bathroom on the other side of the motel room. The light was on inside, emitting an antiseptic florescence that turned Oswaldo's stomach. The stale odor of his body, however, forced him to reconsider.

"Okay," he said. "Let's have a cigarette a first."

* *

Naranja drove a white service van that was parked in a space in front of the motel room. Oswaldo had his cigarette and then showered. This relaxed him enough to take his mind off the pinpoint pain in his upper back, near the shoulders. His head throbbed as well, but he could deal with that general pain. Naranja helped him to the van even though he didn't ask for the assistance. Oswaldo knew he wouldn't last long living like this. He was not used to getting help for anything.

"Okay?" Naranja asked before closing the passenger door.

Oswaldo nodded. Naranja shambled around to the driver's side, and Oswaldo turned back to the rear of the van and scanned the empty space. There were remnants of past travelers: crushed water bottles, a couple of tattered blankets, and a mangy, pink stuffed animal of unknown species.

The van started with a great rumble and pulled out of the motel lot. Texas was only thirty minutes away. They would get into the country illegally through a set point of access arranged by one of Oswaldo's highest-profile associates. These people also used this point of access—among others—for conducting their business, both legal and illicit.

"What's the most you've ever taken across at one time?" Oswaldo asked, nodding to the back of the van.

Naranja covered his eyes with a pair of cheap orange sunglasses.

"I've fit twenty, maybe twenty-five back there before," he said. "I usually have a group I take over, and we cross at night. But you. Well, your situation is not usual."

"How so?"

"You are just one. I guess an important one because I never cross with just one."

"But the other two that didn't make it. That would of made three."

Naranja shrugged.

"One. Three. Same difference. My point is, the back of my van must usually be filled to make any real money."

Oswaldo did not respond.

Naranja kept both hands on the steering wheel. Silence passed between the two men and Oswaldo scanned the unforgiving landscape outside of the van's windows.

"I never thought I'd be back," Oswaldo said,

unprompted. He wasn't sure why he had said it. He almost always kept his thoughts to himself. But something was happening to him now that the disease had hold of him.

"It's difficult with the border patrol, and many of the *Americanos* don't want us there now," Naranja said. "It doesn't really matter for me. I will never live in America. Just work. Always business. But I feel bad for my people sometimes. Dropping them off in a strange place all alone."

Oswaldo thought about his son, Armando. Now that he was this close to El Paso, now that it was real, he had to think about how he'd go about approaching his boy. His son would not want to see him. Oswaldo knew that. He would feel the same way if he were in Armando's position.

The border was two miles ahead. Oswaldo squinted and counted six lanes of cars waiting to cross. Further ahead, the border patrol station was crawling with agents searching for any reason to send the motorists back. Naranja turned off the main road that led to the border. The van rumbled over loose terrain, and its wheels skittered until Naranja gripped the wheel tight.

"You want me to drop you at your mother's house in El Paso, right?" Naranja asked.

Oswaldo thought and shook his head.

"No."

He was not ready to face anyone from his past yet.

Naranja waited for more information until it became clear that Oswaldo would give him none.

"You mean you don't want to go across now?"

"I do," Oswaldo said. "Is there somewhere else safe you could drop me? Somewhere in El Paso?"

Naranja rubbed his chin as he thought. "There is a motel I know of. You have money, right?"

Of course Oswaldo had money. It was *all* he had left.

"Yes."

"I'll take you there, and when you're ready, go see your family."

Oswaldo coughed and looked out of the window.

He saw a place that had faded from his consciousness, and yet was available to his memory as soon as he called upon it. There wouldn't be any tears shed when he set foot in America after all those years. He didn't have time. Tears wouldn't make things right. He wasn't aiming for "right," as nothing would really make it right, not even this final visit. Oswaldo was aiming for something entirely different.

8

THE FIRST DAY OF SCHOOL BROUGHT OPTIMISM for students and athletes alike inside the walls of El Dorado High School. The goofy freshmen staggered around, bumping into upperclassmen who threatened to stuff them inside lockers, while seasoned juniors and seniors congregated at their favorite spots around school: the hidden courtyard for clandestine make-out sessions, and the bowels of the locker room for smoke breaks. The football players ruled the realm of course.

This was Armando's moment. The season was to be his coming-out party, a coronation; and if he so chose, he'd have plenty of opportunity to be a king in the bedroom as well. But his mind was preoccupied with things outside of football.

"What's up, Armando?" asked a random student who passed in the hall.

Armando had never spoken to the student before and assumed that the greeting was the result of his success on the practice field. News of El Dorado's team spread through the halls with the speed and unpredictability of wild fire. It wouldn't be long until the female students came out of the woodwork to test Armando's allegiance to Anna.

Farther down the hall, Anna gathered up her books and went to look for Armando, who hadn't spoken to her since the night of the party at Abuela's house. Anna knew to give him space after the bombshell about his father, yet she also knew that there was a clear fracture in their once airtight relationship. Like Armando, this was a big year for her too. She was taking an entire course load of AP classes, and as if that wasn't daunting enough, she'd be competing in state debate championships that fall. Anna had dreams too. Armando's commitment to her didn't feel as strong as it used to. She, in turn, had to reconsider some decisions that were once forgone conclusions.

Still she loved him.

In the haste of the new season, Armando had not even disclosed his class schedule to Anna. In previous years, she had known his schedule by heart. She knew where he'd be at every moment during the school day and would be there at the drop of a hat to help Armando with a pop quiz or five-paragraph essay. They used to steal kisses during preplanned bathroom breaks. Those days seemed blurry and far away now to Anna.

Armando's focus was compromised on that first morning of school. He wandered through the halls. The questions in his head ran at an infinite loop— *Why is he coming? Why now?*—the most frequent and pressing. What scared him most was allowing the thought of actually wanting to see his father to enter into his mind. Armando was always curious about his father but held too much respect for his mother to ask any questions. *Is it wrong for me to want to see him?*

The mystery surrounding the situation only added to the tension. *Is he actually coming, or is Abuela starting to lose her mind?* Armando wasn't sure, but he knew he would not be able to function like this. He needed structure and repetition in order to succeed. His mother provided the structure at home. Football provided the repetition.

He needed someone to talk to. Someone who had been through something like this. But there was no one. He would have to face this alone, like the many experiences in his life up to that point. He shaved for the first time without learning from his father. He kissed and had sex with his first girl without any lectures from his father. Why would this be any different? He'd never admit it to Anna, but his father's absence played a role in his lukewarm enthusiasm toward having a family of his own in the future.

Anna had both of her parents. This was something he couldn't discuss with her. *What the hell could she possibly understand about abandonment?* And besides, if his father could up and leave him and his mother, maybe it was in him to do the same to Anna? There wasn't anywhere to turn. Armando's mother was there for him, but this was a situation for a man. He did not want Oswaldo in his life. If the moment did come when their paths aligned, he would look the man straight in the eyes and tell him to go back to Mexico.

These thoughts raced through Armando's head as he approached first period. Before he walked into the classroom, there was a tap on his back.

"Howdy stranger," Anna said from behind.

Armando turned around and looked at his girl with soft eyes. He pulled her close and gave her a squeeze. He held her tight and Anna wrapped her arm around his waist.

"How are you?" she whispered.

He didn't respond. He just wanted to hold his girl.

"I," she said. "I can't breathe, baby."

"Sorry," he said, after letting her go.

She smoothed out her blouse and pushed a strand of hair out of her face. "Did you hear anything?"

Armando shook his head.

"Is this your first class? I used to know your entire schedule *before* the first day of school."

Armando didn't say anything as the bell rang and halls cleared. A strange silence descended as they both realized the rift that had formed between them.

"Armando. What's happening to you? What's happening to us?"

"I don't know," he said. "Somehow, though, it feels like it's all slipping away. I don't want it to. But it seems like there's nothing I can do about it."

"Nothing is slipping away. You have it all in your hands. All of it."

"I gotta go, Anna," he said. "First period—"

"I'm gonna come over after practice tonight."

"I don't know if my mom is working a double or not."

"I don't care," she said. "I'm coming."

． ．

At practice after school, Armando let out his frustrations on his defensive teammates. He abused a couple of defensive ends during blocking drills and burned a few linebackers on seam routes during seven-on-seven. The only question on the field was whether or not he could conjure up the focus necessary to dominate.

Before the end of practice scrimmage, the team went through a special teams period. Clark pulled Armando out of these reps because he did not want to overwork his starting tight end.

Armando crouched down on one knee as he watched his teammates execute punt-blocking schemes. He squirted a stream of ice water down the back of his shoulder pads and waited for the sensation to hit. He wiped the sweat off his forehead and gasped. The sun was high. It seared his scalp.

And yet, the urge to get back onto the field consumed him. Being on the field was the only way to push his father's arrival in El Paso out of his mind.

He got off his knee, strapped on his helmet, and trotted onto the field. He took the place of a backup tight end without asking for permission. Clark laughed to himself at the sight, and Committee did the same.

"Sumbitch has a set of stones on him," Committee said.

"Mmm hmm," Clark replied.

Armando blocked the edge during the rest of the special teams period.

The team took a water break before the start of the scrimmage. Armando got back onto a knee, and although he had never prayed for anything in his life, he was willing to try anything to lift the troubles off his shoulders.

Dear Father, I don't ask you for much. But if this is true, please make it untrue. Thanks Father.

Armando crossed himself and raised his head. A whistle shrilled and it was time. The number one offense against the number one defense. Armando stood up and ran into the huddle. Freddie called out the first play of the scrimmage: a simple pass to Armando in the left flat. The huddle broke and all twenty-two players on both sides took their positions. Armando itched as he waited for the snap of the ball. He needed to explode. The ball was snapped, and Armando sprinted into the flat. By the time he whipped his head around, the ball was there. He caught it in stride and instead of trying to avoid the charging strong-side linebacker, Wyatt Ferguson, Armando dipped his right shoulder into the defender's chest. Ferguson bounced off Armando and hit the turf in a heap. Armando continued down the left sideline and outran the entire defense on the way to the end zone. He spiked the ball and stomped his feet like the play had won the state championship game. He could not keep it bottled up inside of him.

On the second play of the scrimmage, it was Armando's job to kick out the defensive end on an off-tackle run to the right. Armando started on the left of the formation before Freddie stomped the ground with his left foot, sending Armando in motion to the right side. The ball was snapped, and Armando put his helmet into the defensive end's chest, driving the defender clear out of the play. Martino took the handoff from Freddie and hit the hole that Armando had created. The play resulted in a forty-yard run. Armando sprinted downfield to where the play had ended and lifted Martino off the turf.

Clark looked over to Committee on the sideline.

"Jesus Christ! We gotta get him to let up on his own guys," Clark said.

Committee looked on.

Freddie came over to Clark for the next play. Clark gave it to him, and Freddie ran back onto the field and into the huddle.

The third play was a pass. All of the eligible receivers on the field were called on to run "nine" routes, or streaks. That meant a seam pattern for Armando. It was his job to read the defense and either run the seam route right down the middle of the field or bend it around the numbers. Before the snap, Armando saw that Dominguez, the middle linebacker, was playing with inside leverage. That clue told Armando to bend his route around the numbers because the linebacker would cut off a straight-line seam route.

On the snap, Armando took a hard jam from the defensive end. After recovering, he looked to see where Dominguez was. Still inside. Armando bent his route to the numbers and when he got enough depth, bent it up the seam. Dominguez carried Armando in coverage for the first few steps, but when both players reached top speed, the linebacker was overmatched. Armando threw his hand up for Freddie. The quarterback saw that there was no safety over the top and released the pass, putting some air under it.

Dammit, Freddie thought, *overthrew it.*

Armando looked up and gauged the ball's trajectory. He pushed his legs into another gear—their final gear—and stretched his arms out as far as they could go. The ball stuck to his fingertips. Armando hauled in the catch and ran into the end zone. Freddie put both palms on his helmet and did not blink, for fear of waking up from this dream season that Armando had spun. Beaten, Dominguez's head hung. Clark's expectations for the offense and for the season as a whole spiked upwards. Committee allowed himself to smile.

Armando squeezed the ball with both hands and screamed at the top of his lungs. There was no specific thought to be conveyed with this primal scream—just emotion. The first three plays of scrimmage were clear illustrations of Armando's physical superiority.

The fourth play would be an illustration of Armando's versatility and, really, a poignant message as to just how far he had come as a football player. His job on this play was to stay on the line of scrimmage and help the offensive line in case of a blitz. If the pocket was clear, he could then leak out into the flat to provide a check-down option for Freddie.

"Let's see if he can pass protect," Clark said to Committee on the sideline.

Committee grunted—his form of agreement.

Armando put his hand in the grass at the end of the line of scrimmage. The strong-side linebacker, Ferguson, showed blitz. Armando could tell because Ferguson's feet were not set. At the snap, Ferguson shot the gap between Armando and the left tackle. The cornerback on that side came on an edge blitz as well. Armando helped the left tackle handle Ferguson and managed to peel back and get just enough of the blitzing cornerback to give Freddie a pocket to step up into. Freddie completed a twenty-yard pass to the right.

Clark clapped his hands.

"Did you see the way he passed off the blitzing backer to Martinez and still got a piece of the blitzing corner?" Clark asked Committee.

Committee nodded.

Jonathan Martinez was El Dorado's All-State left tackle, already committed to Baylor.

"Salguera looked like an offensive lineman there," Clark continued. "We could probably stick him in at left tackle if Martinez ever went down."

"Bite your tongue," Committee said.

Back in the huddle, Martinez and Armando slapped high five.

"Nice job," Martinez said. "You passed it off. Inside out."

Armando nodded. He was pleased with his performance as a blocker on the line of scrimmage though it gave him nowhere near the excitement that catching a pass did. Deep down he hoped this would only be spot duty during the regular season. Armando loved to catch the ball. Although he worked hard in becoming a tight end who could be relied upon to fulfill multiple duties, Armando knew where his true value lay.

The fifth play of the scrimmage was another pass. Clark was giddy with the offensive possibilities that Armando had unlocked with his versatility. So giddy, that he had forgotten about his beloved running game. When Armando got set right before the snap, he quickly realized that the defense was compromised. He could see in its alignment that the middle of the field would be wide open. All he had to do was find the soft spot in the zone and show Freddie his eyes.

On the snap, Armando did just that. He found the soft spot and caught a dart from Freddie in the middle of the field. He was tackled fifteen yards later. When he got up off the turf, he hadn't realized that something had happened back at the line of scrimmage. He could tell by the way the coaches and his teammates were huddled around one player that an injury had occurred.

He ran back to where the ball was snapped and forced his way into the center of the circle of teammates. On the ground in the middle of the circle was left tackle Jonathan Martinez, clutching his left knee while tears streamed down both sides of his face.

9

THAT EVENING, ANNA CAME OVER AFTER ARMANDO got home from practice. She walked into his room and found him in bed with an ice pack wrapped around his left shoulder.

"Hey there, superstar," she said, with a hand on one cocked hip.

"Hey."

"How'd it go out there today?"

"It was good for me. But our left tackle went down. Martinez. He's out for the year. His knee exploded."

Anna winced.

"Poor guy."

"Yeah," Armando said. "I feel so bad for him."

She walked over and sat down on the end of the bed. Armando could smell her hair.

"I didn't see your mom's car out there."

"She's working a double. Won't be home until noon."

In one motion, Anna hopped onto Armando's lower half. In response, he tore off her top. They went at it several times during the course of the night. Anna fell asleep around two a.m. Armando watched her chest rise and fall—a habit of his—until he closed his eyes and drifted away.

· ·

"Pst," Anna whispered.

Armando blinked twice and opened his eyes. Natural light was beginning to creep into the room. Anna nuzzled under Armando's arms. The smell of their sweat dried into the sheets tingled their noses.

"I'm hungry."

"Sleep."

Anna kneed Armando's crotch softly, not that he took any comfort in the fact that it was just a love tap.

"Make your girl breakfast."

"Okay. Okay."

They got out of bed and walked into the kitchen. Armando grabbed the ingredients for Anna's favorite breakfast—blueberry pancakes—and got to work. He eyeballed the milk and prepackaged mix into a large bowl and then cracked a couple of eggs. Anna poured the orange juice as he whisked the batter.

"Have you thought about your father at all?" she asked.

"Whoa, Anna. Where'd that come from? I thought we're having breakfast together."

"We are. I know how tough that night at Abuela's house was for you. I'm just worried about you."

"You know?"

"Yes. I know."

The butter in the frying pan on the stove sizzled

as Armando eyed Anna. He tossed the whisk into the sink, and it splattered the pancake batter.

"The answer is no. I haven't thought about him."

He poured imperfect circles of batter into the frying pan right out of the mixing bowl. The fire was up too high and he regulated the knob to medium heat.

Anna wasn't going to let him shut her out. She had to know what was going on inside her boyfriend's head.

"Well you probably should. I mean, I'm not saying you should worry about it. But if he comes up here to see you—it could be a good thing."

Armando turned away from the stove with spatula in hand and faced Anna.

"A good thing? How? I don't even know him. And he didn't care to know me."

Anna didn't respond. There was hurt in his voice.

"There's nothing good that can come from seeing him," Armando continued. "If he does come, the only reason I'd see him would be to tell him that I don't have a father."

He turned back around and flipped one of the pancakes. It had burned. Armando cursed under his breath.

"You do have a father, Armando. He's still your father."

"No he's not!"

Armando slapped the frying pan off the stove and it crashed onto the kitchen floor. The fire on the stove raged on as Armando approached Anna and loomed. She did not back down however.

"What are you trying to do, Anna? What you are getting at? This isn't one of your books. I'm not a psychology experiment for you to study. This is real life. My life."

"I'm not trying to study you. I'm trying to talk to you. I just think you should consider forgiving him. I think that might make you happier in the long run. That's all."

"Why?" Armando yelled. "Why are you so into me forgiving my father?"

"Baby," she said. "It's because I love you. And I know you're in pain. And that's all it is."

Armando was silent. He watched Anna.

"I won't forgive him."

"Okay, so don't. No one is going to make you. I'm just saying that people make mistakes," she said. "And maybe forgiving him will allow you to let go of the anger you have inside of you."

Armando shook his head.

"His mistake was too big, Anna," Armando said in a low voice before leaving the kitchen and walking upstairs.

Anna turned off the stove, cleaned up the kitchen as best she could, and left Armando's house.

. . . .

Committee called Armando into his office before first period the next morning. When Armando arrived,

Clark was there as well. They moved into a conference room in the athletic center where both the lighting and acoustics were better.

Clark and Armando sat next to one another, adjacent to Committee, who sat at the head of a long conference room table.

"How's the shoulder?" Clark asked Armando.

"It's fine. Just a little sore."

"We got official word on Martinez," Clark said. "Torn ACL, among other damaged ligaments. Out for the season."

Committee hadn't spoken a word yet. And it was then that Armando realized that the head coach of the team didn't have much say in things. It was common knowledge that Clark ran the offensive side of the ball, but Armando thought that injuries, particularly a serious injury to a player the caliber of Martinez, should at the very least evoke comment from the head coach.

"We've been impressed with you, Armando,"

Clark said. "The way you worked on your body in the off-season. The way you've learned the playbook."

Clark pointed to his head.

"Thanks Coach."

"What I'm about to ask you is difficult," Clark added.

Armando looked at Committee, who was staring straight ahead. A helpless feeling washed over him. He felt alone and unprotected.

"We want to switch you to left tackle for this season," Clark said. "We think you are the best option to fill Martinez's place as our starting left tackle."

The air went out of Armando's chest. His first instinct was to cry. He shook his head repeatedly as if the action alone would negate what his coach had just said.

"But Coach. I'm a tight end. "I'm not—"

Armando looked into his coach's eyes.

Clark did not blink, although it was a hard task.

"I'm a tight end," Armando repeated. "I'm not a tackle. I'm a tight end."

"You're a hell of a tight end," Clark replied. "Probably the best tight end in the state. And you're a hell of a person too. That's why this is so hard. But you're a luxury we can't afford. Without a strong left tackle, our offense just can't work. We wouldn't even be able to throw the ball to you without a left tackle."

"You can't find another lineman to fill in?" Armando asked.

"You are the strongest candidate to be that dominant left tackle for us, Armando," Clark said.

Armando felt a warm swirl of sickness in his stomach. He gripped the hand rests of his chair and held on tight.

"You are good enough to make the switch. I saw it in practice yesterday. On that one play where you and Martinez worked together on the blitz pickup. It was seamless and you had never worked on it live before. I believe you can save our season, son," Clark said.

"But Coach, I'm a tight end."

Clark and Committee looked at one another. They had been at this long enough to know that the sell wouldn't be an easy one. Clark sighed but not out of discouragement.

"We're asking you to sacrifice, Armando. For your teammates. For your coaches. For the entire school. We can win state with you at left tackle."

Armando did not respond. Clark was calm and watched his star tight end with understanding eyes. He sympathized with Armando, understood the work the young man had to put in to gain expertise as a tight end. But his conviction was strong. The team needed Armando to make the switch.

"I know you're upset. And I know it's hard. But this is an opportunity to sacrifice for the team," Clark said. "We are a running team. With you at left tackle we can be a dominant running team."

"I'm a tight end," Armando said again. "I have a dream. It only comes true if I'm at tight end."

"We win state with you making this sacrifice," Clark said, "and your dream will come true. You'll have the opportunity to go back to tight end for your senior season. But the commitment you'd have shown your teammates will be more important than any statistic."

Armando thought but was in no shape to make a determination on the spot.

"What if I don't want to make the switch?"

"It's your decision," Clark said. "We won't make you switch."

Clark and Committee stood up in tandem and left the conference room. The pressure of the decision rested heavily on Armando's shoulders.

10

AFTER THE INITIAL SLEDGEHAMMER OF CLARK'S proposal wore off, Armando calmed himself and went to class. During lunch, he went to see Clark and Committee once again to ask for a couple of days to think about the position switch. The coaches decided to allow Armando one day to mull it over because the offense needed to get acclimated to the new left tackle—Armando or otherwise—in preparation for the first game of the season. Armando accepted and left school with Anna. Either way, Armando was expected to be on the field for practice after school the next day.

"Why does it matter what position you play?" Anna asked, as they sat in his car, he in the driver's seat, she in the passenger's. "I mean, if you're good you're good, right? Being *on* the field is what it's about, right?"

"You don't understand."

"I don't understand football or I don't understand you?"

Armando stared straight ahead.

"I don't know," he said.

"See," she said. "This is what I was talking about. You're slipping through my fingers and there's nothing I can do about it."

"Anna, enough! I think I need to be alone right now. I have to think about this. I have to think about everything."

"You don't want me to come with you?"

"No."

"Fine."

Anna unbuckled her seatbelt.

"Let me ask you something," she said, her eyes

shiny. "Do you need to think about us? Are you and I something that you need to think about?"

Armando didn't reply.

Anna got out of the car. She leaned in the window and stared at Armando.

"Just go," she said.

He started the car and pulled away without saying goodbye. She watched his car get smaller until it was gone.

In the car, Armando called his cousin Raul. Raul was finishing up at work and agreed to meet Armando at the park in a half hour. With a bit of time to spare, Armando drove over to Gabriel's for six *carne asada* tacos before heading over to the park. He left his car in a spot near the tree at the edge of the park.

"What's up, *carnal*?" Raul asked, as he approached Armando sitting underneath the tree.

Armando stood and the two cousins hugged.

"My coaches are jeopardizing things for me, that's what," Armando said.

"What's up?"

"They asked me to switch to left tackle for the season. Jon Martinez tore up his knee and they want me to fill his spot."

Raul waited for the bad news but in his mind, it never came.

"And?" he finally asked.

"And what? They want me to move from tight end. They said I should sacrifice for the good of the team and play left tackle. But I don't want to. My dream is to make it to the NFL as a tight end."

What Raul was about to say to his cousin was difficult. But it needed to be said.

"Look," Raul said, before a deep breath. "I love you like a brother. But you're being a whiny little bitch right now."

Armando looked at his cousin with disbelief. He thought that Raul would have his back.

"They are talking about *starting* you at left tackle, right?"

"Yeah." Armando said.

"So what are you complaining about? You're

starting, right? Do your thing at left tackle and you'll get a scholarship. Who cares what position it's at?"

"You don't get it," Armando shot back. "Why am I even talking to you about this? You've never played football. You've never stepped out on that field."

Raul perked up even though his younger cousin was double his size.

"What do you think? Just because I've never played football, that makes you better than me?"

Armando didn't reply.

"That's right," Raul said. "I've been sacrificing my whole life while you've been out there on *that* field. When we were kids, while you were out playing a game, I was out working to help my mom with the bills. I never had a father either, remember?"

Armando put his head down. He couldn't meet his older cousin's glare because shame had gripped him tight.

"But maybe I'm the wrong person to ask since you know it all," Raul said. "But if you want my advice, go ask your mother about sacrifice. Because without her working as hard as she does, you wouldn't be able to play the game you love."

Raul left Armando standing underneath the tree. He got into his car and left. Armando, stunned, waited for Raul's car to disappear before getting into his own. He started it up and drove away from the park. After a few blocks, he pulled over to the side of the road. He thought about what his mother went through after his dad took off. A few minutes of silence passed before Armando fired the engine back up and pulled the car back onto the road.

. . . .

It didn't matter what anyone said. Armando's dream was on life support. None of it added up. *Why are things breaking this way for me?* All he wanted to do was play the game he loved and push his talent as far as it could go. First the news about his dad. Then the position switch.

"What did I do to deserve this?" he asked aloud as he drove around El Paso.

He didn't want anyone else's opinions. He couldn't go to his mother or his uncle Gus because they both worked so hard. He didn't want to put any more burden on them. The next move was his. When Armando thought of where to go to do his thinking, only one place came to mind. He drove over to Album Park in east El Paso, the place where he first played organized football at ten years old.

The ten-minute drive to Album Park brought back all kinds of memories for Armando—memories that ranged from nervous uncertainty to pure joy. He remembered sitting in the back of his uncle Gus's pickup truck on the way to practice. When Armando first started playing, he disliked hitting so much that he thought he'd never make it. He played the minimum that every child was mandated to play during those first couple of seasons, and in that time span felt no connection to the game. Armando didn't know why he was out there in the first place. The game contained so much confrontation, called for such aggression, and none of it came natural to him.

Yet his mother and his uncle Gus would not let him quit in those early years. They thought that being on a team with other kids his age, who were pulling for the same common goal, was a good thing. Connie and Gus wanted Armando to be a part of something that was bigger than himself. They also wanted him to develop a sense of responsibility, so he wouldn't end up like his father, Oswaldo.

Then things turned one day for Armando early in his third season of playing football. He was thirteen years old and tired of simply being on the team. There was a kid on the team named Trent, the one that everyone else on the team feared. He was the hardest hitter on the team. He was such a hard hitter that the very utterance of his name was enough to intimidate. Trent caused the timid players on the team to rethink their decisions to play football.

Armando was tired of taking hits. He wanted to know what it felt like to dish them out. On that transformative day, early in the season, Armando volunteered to go up against Trent in a "nutcracker" drill when no one else on the team dared. What came next was the biggest moment of Armando's life up to that point. After Trent nailed him on the first rep, Armando realized that the hit hadn't killed him. He wasn't afraid anymore. He bounced up off the field and implored his coach to give him another shot at Trent. This second rep was marked by a thunderclap of historic proportions. After the dust settled on this rep, Trent was the one on his back. Armando held out his hand to help Trent up. Although jarred, Trent reached up and gripped Armando's hand tight. That was the first time Armando looked Trent in the eye, and it felt good. Armando was a football player from that moment on.

But here was Armando, at a crossroads again, at the same place where his football life nearly ended and then truly began. Armando parked his car in the lot right next to the field where the "nutcracker" event had occurred. He looked onto the field, as little kids passed by in oversized shoulder pads and helmets. He noticed the fathers standing behind their sons. Armando had to admit that there something nice in that mixture of football, fathers, and sons. Many of his teammates over the seasons had their fathers behind them. Missing his never meant as much as it did in that moment. The unprocessed feelings related to his father's betrayal swelled inside his chest and threatened to explode his heart.

Overwhelmed, he got out of his car and approached the field as the pee-wee team on it began to stretch. By the looks of it, the team was made up of nine-year-olds—that age where the energy is off the charts and the hits aren't anywhere near vicious. A few of the fathers on the sideline recognized Armando as an El Dorado player and wondered why an important player on the team was at a pee-wee practice. Shouldn't he be at practice? Wasn't the first game of the season coming up?

The team out on the field finished stretching and made its way over to the head coach standing at midfield. Armando observed the young coach as he interacted with his players. Over time, Armando had become adept at figuring out his coaches. He knew when they were genuine and when they were not. To him, Committee was neither. The old man was a simple non-entity. By sharp contrast, Armando saw Clark as genuine. Now as he again contemplated the offer to change positions and placed it in the context of the good of the team, Armando could feel his once dug-in stance begin to soften. That didn't mean that his mind was made up, though.

Armando believed in signs. They didn't have to come from God. But he needed *something* from *somewhere* to reassure him that changing from tight end to left tackle would work out for him. And to a greater and more remote extent, Armando needed to know that he was going to be alright if his father showed up out of nowhere after fifteen years.

On the field in front of him were no such signs. At least not at first glance. The nine-year-olds stumbled through the simplest of drills. The coach's basic message was for each player to give it their all for the person next to them. Who knew if the message resonated with them? But the coach was undaunted and continued spreading his message regardless of whether or not his players could grasp it, because that's what coaches do. The good ones at least.

The coach's message to his pee-wee team did not constitute a sign.

Armando kicked a clod of dirt and cursed underneath his breath.

He had almost given up until a sudden commotion came from the field. The head coach barked with excitement after the effort displayed by one of the squad's smallest players. The event occurred during a blocking drill called "capture the flag." The kid being praised was a running back, and his helmet looked to be so ill fitting that it resembled a beach ball bobbing through the air. Armando got closer to get a better look.

The entire team was buzzing now, another sensation that Armando knew well. When one player makes an inspiring play, it leads to more and more inspiring plays from others, and then before you know it, you have got yourself a team to be reckoned with. The miniature running back, who had just dispatched a player a little bigger than he was, was now put up against a player that was double his size. In the drill, it was the larger player's job to get through the running back and capture the white flag that symbolized the quarterback.

The coach had an inkling that the small running back would most likely stay small. If the player held dreams of elevating to higher levels of football, he'd have to get used to hitting players that were much bigger than he was.

The two players, one small and one big, got into their stances.

"Go!" the young head coach yelled.

The larger player went with a bull rush, thinking there was no way that the small running back had the strength to stop him. The running back took two quick steps back and then launched himself at the chest of the larger player. Their pads popped harmlessly in Armando's eyes, but in the eyes of everyone on the field, the collision was major league. Once again, the small running back had blocked a bigger player. "Block" was the wrong word. "De-cleat" was a better one.

The running back squeezed past his jubilant teammates and went over to the larger player with his hand held out. The smaller player was as eager to put the larger one on the turf as he was to help his fallen teammate to his feet afterward. And though it *wasn't* the exact sign Armando was looking for, it was enough. He didn't need any more reasons to love football. They were all over the place, right there on that field.

II

OSWALDO WAS AS RESTED AND RECOVERED AS A man in his condition could hope to be, after spending two nights in the motel just across the border in El Paso. His cancer was under control, aside from the violent coughing fit he had experienced during the first night in the motel. On his third day back in America, Oswaldo gathered his cigarettes and money and checked out of the hotel. First, he stopped at a clothing store to buy some essentials—socks, underwear—as well as a new outfit. Oswaldo loved the tautness and smell of a brand new pair of snake skin boots, so he indulged. The boots clicked greedily on the sidewalk as he walked away from the store.

The plan was to go to see his mother, Armando's *abuela*, first. That made the most sense. The old woman would surely know where to find Armando and would most likely give that information to Oswaldo after the initial shock wore off. All those years ago, he hadn't even told his mother that he was leaving to go back to Mexico. But the way he saw it, he couldn't have told anyone in the States. His silent departure to Mexico protected everyone who was connected to him in El Paso: Connie, his mother, and most of all, his baby boy, Armando.

When Oswaldo reached into his pocket and pulled out a slip of paper, the address matched the house he was standing in front of. He couldn't walk up to the door right away. He needed a cigarette first. He paced as he smoked, and the cigarette calmed him as much as it was going to.

He stared at his mother's door and the indecision swelled.

"*Carajo*," he muttered.

Oswaldo thought about turning around, leaving America, and heading back to Mexico. It would be easy to forget about all this. He could go somewhere and die alone and leave these people be. These people who had their own lives *without* him. But inside his decaying chest, there was a heart that beat for redemption. A heart that was once one of the blackest in all of Mexico, was determined to seek out its redemption with the only person that mattered to him now. He could die at any time. But he would not die comfortably unless he saw his boy.

He walked up to his mother's front door and softly knocked three times. After nothing happened, he knocked three more times, loudly. Heavy footsteps approached the door and then, the door was cracked opened.

"*Mama?*"

Abuela opened the door wide.

He recognized her face instantly though it was

ravaged by age. The old woman recognized him as well. Instead of saying something, anything, she simply wept. She pulled her son into the house and put her arms around him. He couldn't say anything either but shed no tears. He hugged his mother, and as she buried her face into his midsection, Oswaldo scanned the pictures hanging on the wall next to the front door. His eyes set on a picture of a young man about the age of fifteen. The boy wore an American football uniform. He was large. The boy's eyes reminded Oswaldo of his own. That was his sign. The boy in the picture was his son, Armando.

"*Mijo*," she said finally.

"*Mama.*"

Oswaldo took his mother by the hand and walked over to the picture of Armando. He looked up to it and her eyes followed.

"Is that?"

"*Sí.*"

"He's big."

"You should see him now."

Oswaldo and his mother were in the kitchen. After a minute or two, she presented a tray holding two cups of coffee, cream, sugar and sweets. Oswaldo remembered that his mother made a good cup of coffee; he hadn't had good coffee since being back in America.

"*No azucar, si*?

"*Si, Mama.*"

She had remembered after all those years how her son took his coffee. Her memory had corroded in recent years but this detail flashed into her head on first sight of her son sitting at the kitchen table. She dug a little deeper and unearthed another gem; Oswaldo hated *all* things sweet. She quickly pulled the tray holding the sweet stuff off the table, and mother and son focused on the coffee instead.

They were silent for a moment as they sipped. The shock had worn off, the tears dried away. Now it was time to really talk. Oswaldo got the same feeling as when he was called in for a job by his associates. After the pleasantries, it was time for business.

"What brought you back here, my son?"

Oswaldo took a sip of coffee and a drag from his cigarette.

"I came to see my son, Mama," he said. "Armando."

Her eyes welled up again at the mention of her grandson. Armando was, of course, her favorite out of all the grandchildren. From the moment her son left, she and Armando shared a ubiquitous sadness that stemmed from their common loss. She lost a son and he lost a father. A relationship between Abuela and *nieto* sprouted from that understanding, and after years had passed and tears were shed, that understanding grew into genuine love.

"Why did you leave?"

"I can't get into that now," he said. "I just need to see my son. Will you help me?"

She sighed and a tear fell down her left cheek.

Despite it all, she still loved her son. But before

that day when Oswaldo knocked on her door, that love had been a conflation—a fierce, protective love she showered on Armando, a love that was derived from Oswaldo. She closed her eyes and decided that those boundaries were no longer necessary. The distinctions could now be tossed aside.

"You don't have to answer my questions, *mijo*," she said. "But you will have to answer his."

"Yes."

"El Dorado High School."

"Thank you, Mama."

12

ARMANDO WALKED INTO COMMITTEE'S OFFICE early before school the next morning and was not surprised to find Clark there too.

"Armando. Good morning," Clark said. "Wanna sit?"

Armando sat down in front of his two coaches and waited for Clark to begin. When a few moments of silence passed, Armando inhaled deeply and exhaled even deeper.

"I'll do the position switch," Armando said. "I don't want to. But if it helps the team, I'll do it."

Clark nodded.

"That's fantastic, Armando," Clark said. "Thank you. It means a lot."

Committee smiled.

"But can you do one thing for me?" Armando asked.

"Shoot," Clark said.

"When you guys talk to scouts, can you sell me as a tight end? That's the position I would like to play in college."

"Of course," Clark said. "But I think I wouldn't be doing my job if I didn't alert you to the possibility of you being great at left tackle. It's the single most important position on offense if you ask me. Anyway, you have the size, speed, and ability to get a scholarship at any position you play. And I mean that."

"Thank you," Armando said. "But still, if you can, please sell me as a tight end. I have my reasons."

"Okay," Clark said.

Armando released another deep sigh. A weight had

been lifted off his shoulders. Not the entire weight, but a start nonetheless.

"We're gonna help you, Armando," Clark said. "We're gonna help you get to where you want to go."

Armando nodded.

"It's going to look great to colleges that you were willing to sacrifice for the team," Clark added.

Armando stood up, shook his coaches' hands and left the office.

Clark looked over to Committee.

"We have to do right by him," Clark said.

"I'm gonna make some calls to UT and Texas Tech, maybe Baylor too," Committee said importantly.

"I'll put in some calls as well," Clark said.

· ·

Anna waited for Armando outside of the cafeteria during lunch. He arrived with a long face. Her face slumped as well.

"Hi baby," she said. They kissed. "You okay?"

"I went to talk to the coaches this morning," he said. "I decided to do it."

"You don't look happy about it."

"When I first left Coach's office after letting them know, I felt good. All that talk about giving yourself up for the benefit of others is real. Not just some slogan. But after first period, I started feeling sad again."

"About the position change?"

"No, I don't think so."

Anna knew what was bothering Armando now, but she didn't want to go back down that path.

"Let's not eat in there today," she said. "It's nice outside."

"I have to get some food," he said, nodding to the cafeteria door.

"You can have my lunch," she said. "I'm not hungry."

They walked out of school and toward the football field. They took a spot midway up the bleachers.

"Talk to me," Anna said.

"I don't know. Ever since I got the news about my father, there's been something hanging over me. I planned for this season to be big. I dreamed big."

"What is your dream?"

Armando looked at Anna. He had never told her—the person who was supposed to be the most important in his life—what his dream was.

"I want to make it to the NFL. I want to play tight end in the NFL."

"My dream is to be with you forever, and one day have a family together," she said softly and looked away.

"That's your dream? With your brains you could do anything you want. And your biggest dream is to have a family with me?"

"How can we stay together if we go to different colleges?" she asked. "You'll probably end up at some college in Texas, and my first choice wouldn't be to stay in Texas for college. But I would do it if that meant we could be together."

"Staying in Texas would be a joke for you. You belong somewhere in the Ivy League."

"What are you saying, Armando?"

"I'm not saying anything," he said. "I'm just thinking."

Anna was silent now. They both were. She was disturbed by the outright uncertainty Armando displayed. She knew that things hadn't been going well between them. They hadn't in a long while. But she could not picture her life without him and she had always known that Armando felt the same.

No matter what happened Anna had never allowed herself to think about breaking up with Armando. Until now.

"Do you want to break up?" she asked. "Is that what you want?"

Armando was long in answering.

"No," he said quietly, breathless. "That's not what I want. But maybe until things cool off with football and my dad . . . "

Anna waited, incessantly tapping her right foot on the bleacher.

"We should take a little break," he said.

"A break?"

"Yeah. We've never experienced other people. You're the only girl I've even been with. I'm sure you feel the same way. Don't you want to, at the very least, go out on a date with another guy?"

That did it. Anna's face broke and she stood up from the bleacher.

"So that's what this is about?" she screamed. "This pathetic charade you're keeping up about your father and changing positions. This crap about keeping your dream alive. It's all about sleeping with other girls."

"No. No. Anna. I don't mean it that way. I just . . . "

Anna turned her back and walked away from Armando. The tears started to come as she descended the stairs and reached the field.

Armando stood up.

"Anna!" he shouted. "Anna! Come back!"

She didn't stop nor turn around. Armando watched until she disappeared into the school.

Armando sat back down and punched the bleacher with his right hand, sending a shock throughout his entire arm.

. . . .

"What the hell happened?" the trainer asked in the locker room before practice.

"Nothing," Armando said. "Just banged it somewhere."

The trainer examined the hand, squeezing it at certain points in an attempt to trigger a reaction.

"Ah," Armando said. "Yeah, right there."

The trainer observed that exact spot. He massaged the tissue away from the bone.

"It's not broken," the trainer said. "You just did a number on it."

Armando pulled his hand back and tried to flex the pain out of it.

"I wish you would tell me how you did it," the trainer said.

"It's fine."

The trainer wrapped the hand tightly. Suiting up one-handed was a bit of a struggle for Armando, but he managed it. What gave him pause was that he had to get through an entire full-contact practice with one hand, at a position that he had never played before, no less.

Armando was in a faraway place out on the field right before practice. His hand throbbed underneath its bandage, and his mind was equally riddled with confusion. The rest of his teammates were joking around and boasting about their achievements with various girls around school. Armando was just trying to keep his mind off of Anna and his father. After a little while, Freddie walked over, helmet off and with a ball in his hand.

"What's up?" Freddie asked. "What happened yesterday? Coach Clark said that you weren't feeling good and couldn't make it to practice."

"Something like that," Armando said, gripping his right hand.

Armando eyed Freddie to see if he knew.

"Did you hear?"

"Hear what?"

"They asked me to move to left tackle after Jon went down."

Freddie's mouth dropped.

Armando shrugged. "They said I should sacrifice for the team and that we have a better chance to win state if our running game is dominant."

"Have you ever played tackle before?"

"No."

"That's why you weren't at practice then?"

"Yeah. I needed to think it over."

"What, they gave you a choice?"

"Yeah."

"And you agreed to make the switch?"

Armando nodded.

"Damn," Freddie said.

"That's not all."

"What?"

"Me and Anna split."

Freddie shook his head.

"Can't catch a break," Armando said.

"Did you want to split with her?"

"No," he said. "I mean, I'm not sure. I mentioned that maybe we should just take a break. But I didn't mean that I wanted it to be over."

Freddie squeezed the ball with both hands.

"Sorry, man," he said. "Maybe you can find some peace out here. I know I do."

Freddie looked out to the field and Armando's eyes followed. He hoped that Freddie was right. Football was hard enough to play with a clear head. Now that Armando's head was a train wreck, all bets were off. Anything was possible at this point. A season full of promise was now hanging by a thread.

He closed his eyes and took a deep breath. Committee blew his whistle and practice began. There was no grandiose announcement to the team about the big position switch. The team would find out when Armando went with the offensive lineman to hit the sled, instead of catching passes from Freddie with the rest of the receivers.

After the team stretched, another whistle sounded and marked the first time in Armando's high school career that he wasn't a tight end. He watched the other tight ends with envy while he waited in line for a blocking drill. The new starter at tight end was a sophomore named Cam McIntosh. McIntosh had some size and leaping ability but nowhere near Armando's combination of bulk and speed.

Armando shook his head as McIntosh caught a seam route from Freddie.

"Come on, Salguera!" a voice yelled out. "Get your head out of your ass!"

The voice came from El Dorado's offensive line coach, Sean Offit, an ex-cop, ex-Division III offensive lineman, a squat little guy who always sported a bottom lip stuffed with dip. Armando had crossed paths with Offit before because tight ends were no strangers to blocking drills. But he had never dealt with Offit before as his primary position coach.

"Come on pretty boy, Salguera!" Offit droned. "You can catch all those passes like a prima donna, but can you play down in the trenches with the big boys?"

"My bad, Coach."

Armando's first drill as an offensive lineman was a one-on-one blocking drill with a very simple purpose. It was him against a defensive lineman, and his goal was to drive the defender off the ball. The defensive player's goal was just as simple: push Armando into the backfield.

"Set hut!" Offit yelled.

Armando shot up out of his three-point stance, and as soon as he made contact with the defender, his right hand seared. The defender took advantage and drove Armando into the backfield.

"See?" Offit said. "It's not easy. Gotta have better hand placement."

Armando knew all about hand placement. The problem was he only had one useful hand.

"Let me go again," Armando said.

"Get your ass up there then!"

Armando lined up across from the same defender and this time planned on punching with his left hand. By using his good hand, he'd be able to gain control of the defender while protecting the injured one. The only part of his right arm that was available for use was the forearm. It was spared by the punch to the bleacher, and he could use it to drive the defender back.

Both players got into three-point stances.

"Set hut!"

Armando got a decent initial punch and stunned the defender off the line of scrimmage. His hand plan worked; he gained initial control and then drove the defender back with his right forearm. His hand was fine after the rep.

"Yeah!" Offit yelled. "Ata-baby! You might be useful yet, Salguera."

Armando went to the back of the line and, without even thinking about it, began staring at the receivers again. He did this until he reached the front of the blocking drill, and Offit gave him an earful again.

. . . .

The next challenge for Armando was the nine-on-seven drill, where the offense tried to impose its will on the defense by hammering it with running plays only. The entire offensive coaching staff came together for this drill, and Clark made his way over to Armando right before the offense broke the huddle prior to the first play.

"How are you holding up?" Clark asked.

"I'm fine, Coach."

"Yeah?"

"Yeah."

"We're coming right behind you on this one."

The huddle broke, and Armando took his position on the end of the line. Everything had a similar look from that vantage point. But the execution and footwork were much different. The most glaring difference was that instead of a lot of double-team blocks, which is what Armando was used to as a tight end, he would be expected to execute more one-on-one blocks.

Freddie called out his cadence and snapped the ball. Armando was slow off the line, and the defender in front of him put both hands into his chest and eventually knocked him into the backfield. El Dorado's starting tailback, Howard Martino, ran right into Armando's back and the play lost five yards.

"Well, that was a mess," Clark said to Committee from behind the play. "Okay offense, huddle up!"

As Armando peeled himself off the turf, a wave of self-consciousness hit him. Just a few days before, he was lighting practice up and now this? What would people around school think of him now? Throw in the fact that he was alone after breaking up with Anna, and it all seemed like too much to bear.

Armando joined the huddle late. His teammates

stared at him as he flexed his right hand. Clark pulled Armando aside.

"First play," Clark said. "No biggie."

"I was late off the ball," Armando said.

"It's a little different. You gotta be more aggressive. When you're at tight end, there's more room for finesse as a blocker. That's not the case when you're at tackle."

Offit was screaming at the rest of the offensive line as Clark spoke with Armando about the first play. Armando appreciated Clark's discreet coaching style more than he did Offit's.

"Got it."

"Don't forget to use your hands," Clark said. "It's a lot. But you'll get it."

Armando nodded.

"The trainer said your hand was bothering you. Are you alright?"

"It's fine."

Freddie called out the play in the huddle, and the offensive line approached the ball. As Armando lowered himself into a three-point stance, his only focus was to gain an early advantage on the defender. The ball was snapped, and this time Armando fired out of his stance. The defender had no chance as Armando rooted him out of the hole and drove him into the ground. Martino ran for twenty yards through the hole he had created. Armando knew he risked injury by punching with his right hand, but he didn't care. It was worth it. Offit went crazy, running over and slapping Armando on the back of the helmet. Teammates congratulated him on his first successful play as an offensive lineman.

When Armando got back to the huddle, Freddie and Clark were waiting for him. Freddie gave him a high-five and a pat on the helmet. Clark patted him on the back. It felt good.

By the end of Armando's first practice as the starting left tackle of El Dorado High, he'd had his share of ups and downs. Armando was the true definition of a work in progress. His body was beat up as well. His shoulder was raw from the extra blocking, and his right hand would need to be managed.

Armando felt good being out there with the team again though. He was the last player on the field because Offit wanted to go over a couple of things with him. Armando didn't mind. He was never afraid of a little extra work.

When his practice day was finally finished, a man dressed in white appeared near the entrance to the locker room. The man had the same skin complexion as him, and when Armando looked at the man's face, he knew.

"What the?" Armando said.

The man stood in place. He didn't look like a man of advanced age, but the frailty of his body gave off that impression. The man's eyes however did not match his sorry physical stature. The eyes neither held fear nor confusion.

"Armando," the man said.

"Oswaldo?"

"*Si.*"

The two just stared at each other for a while. Armando was all alone with his father. All of his coaches and teammates were in the locker room.

"I heard you were coming. Abuela said so. I wasn't sure if I even believed her. The fear was there anyway."

Oswaldo couldn't speak. He licked his lips many times to speak but no words followed.

"I don't know why you came," Armando said, "but . . ." He stopped. "Look, I gotta go. I have to shower and change." He turned his back on Oswaldo.

"Son," Oswaldo said quietly.

Armando turned around and glared at Oswaldo. He couldn't believe that this man had the balls to use *that* word.

"Can we talk after you are done washing up?"

Armando was unable to hide the disgust on his face.

"Talk? Talk about what?"

"I don't expect you to want to see me," he said. "But please . . ."

Armando took a deep breath. His eyes watered but no tears fell. He could not show himself to be weak in front of this man.

"Give me twenty minutes," Armando said. "I'll meet you up on the bleachers."

Oswaldo nodded submissively.

Armando walked into to the locker room, and Oswaldo prepared for the coughing fit that'd follow his ascent up the bleachers.

· ·

Oswaldo smoked two full cigarettes and lit a third while he waited at the top of the bleachers. The cigarettes didn't calm him; there was no chemical answer for the jitters he felt. Armando approached, staring at him the entire time as he ascended the stairs. It was then that Oswaldo realized what kind of physical specimen his son was. These details were swallowed up by the shock of actually seeing his son again. However, his feeling of pride was enveloped by a look of anger and disgust on son's face.

"Put that out. I hate cigarettes."

Oswaldo put the cigarette out at once.

"Make this quick. I don't have a lot of time for you."

"Will you sit?"

Armando parked himself and left some space between them.

Oswaldo stared straight ahead, and Armando continued to glare at him.

"What do you want?" Armando asked finally.

Oswaldo gave no response. He did, however, turn to look at his son.

Armando stared straight into his father's eyes, almost menacingly. "I said, what do you want? What's the matter, you don't speak English? Abuela says your English is good. That's always great to hear. I love hearing my *abuela* tell stories about you."

Armando's breathing was feral now. He could feel his back start to arch, and the muscles in his arms begin to contract. The pain in his right hand was numbed by the adrenaline coursing through his body.

"I . . ." Oswaldo said. "I came to see you."

"I know you came to see me. But what do you *want*?"

"I'm . . . I'm very sick. I don't have much time left."

Armando shot up and towered over his father. "You're sick? Really? That's too bad. Do you know how many times I've been sick over the past fifteen years? And where were you?"

Oswaldo shook his head and his eyes watered. No tears fell.

"You know what? I don't care if you die right now. Right up here."

Armando turned to leave and Oswaldo stood up. "Please. Don't leave, son."

Armando turned around with rage in his eyes, a rage that never made its way onto the football field. Oswaldo crumpled face-first into the bleachers.

Armando lunged forward and set the old man on his feet. Oswaldo felt like skin and bones in Armando's strong hands. Oswaldo gripped his son's huge biceps.

"This is the first time I've touched you in fifteen years," Oswaldo whispered.

Armando let out a deep breath.

"If you don't tell me what you want, I'm going to let go of you, and you'll never see me again. Please, don't waste my time," Armando said.

"I'm dying. Cancer is all over my body. Once the doctor told me, I knew the last thing I wanted to do was see you."

Armando pulled away. Oswaldo wobbled a bit but was able to stand on his own two feet. As hard as he tried, Armando couldn't help the warm flood that pooled in his eyes.

"Well you've seen me. And this is all you get."

"Please, son," Oswaldo said. "Please. I just want to look at you. I want to be near you before I die."

Armando wiped tears from his eyes before taking another deep breath. His breathing sped up, along with his heart rate. Armando focused to regulate his breaths. His chest expanded and receded. Expanded and receded. After one more controlled and deep breath, Armando shook his head.

"No. This is all you get."

Armando left Oswaldo and walked down the stairs without turning back.

Oswaldo tried not to focus on his son's response to his reemergence. He lit a cigarette with a shaky hand and began replaying the moment of seeing his son for the first time in fifteen years.

13

AFTER THE ENCOUNTER WITH HIS FATHER, ARMANDO went by Anna's house to see if she would talk to him. She wasn't home. He tried calling her that night, but she wouldn't pick up. He then sent five texts with no response. Usually, when Anna was angry at him about something, she'd answer the phone just to tell him to screw off. He had really pissed this one away. He needed her now more than ever, and she wasn't there *because* of him.

. . . .

The next morning at school, Armando looked all over the halls for Anna before first bell. She wasn't in her first-period class, and he wasn't able to check her second-period class because his second-period teacher would not let him use the bathroom. The news of their breakup had spread throughout school, though Armando heard no whispers as he went from class to class. He eschewed lunch, his favorite "period," to wait by her locker instead.

She finally approached, clutching her binder with both arms.

"You weren't in first period."

"So what do you care? I got to school late," she shot back.

"You never get to school late."

"What do you want?"

"I want to talk."

"We can't talk anymore."

"I didn't say that I wanted us to end."

"You don't have any *say* anymore."

"Come on, Anna," Armando said as he put his arm around her waist.

She pulled away violently, her eyes wild.

"Since you're a football star now, why don't you see if any of these little girls around school will have you. I'm sure you'll learn a lot from screwing a bunch of girls who know absolutely nothing about you."

"You can't burn me for no reason, Anna," he said. "I didn't do anything wrong. I never cheated on you. I was just thinking out loud."

"You can't cheat on me because we're not together anymore."

"Listen, I know I've been distant, what with football and the news of my dad coming up. That was hard on me. I was confused. I was going through a lot—still am. I need you now."

"Too bad."

Armando knew from their other little breakups that Anna's anger could reach uncontrollable levels. But this was different. There was a razor's edge to this. He wasn't sure he could talk himself back into her arms.

"My dad is here."

Her eyes softened then returned to skepticism.

"Where?"

"El Paso."

"How long have you known?"

"Since yesterday. He ambushed me right after practice."

There was silence.

"Can we take a walk?" Armando asked.

Anna looked up at the ceiling, shook her head and took a deep breath through her mouth.

"Yeah. But not for long."

· ·

"What are you gonna do?" Anna asked as they walked across El Dorado's field in back of school.

"Nothing."

"Why are you talking to me about it then?"

"I thought it was important that you know I saw my father for the first time in fifteen years."

"Okay. I get that. You saw him. Now what?"

"Like I said. Nothing. Why are you giving me such a hard time?"

Anna stopped and put her hand on her head.

"Because I can't deal with this anymore. You don't talk to me. You ignore me. You shut me out. Then you basically tell me you want to be with other girls. And your dad comes into town, and you come to me to talk? Like I can help? Now? You've built your dream without me. And you're right, now it's time for me to go after mine. So, good luck with your football and your father. I don't have to deal with this anymore because we're not together."

"What the hell, Anna? Are you really gonna do this right now? At this moment?"

"I'm not doing anything."

Now Armando was the one with the crazy eyes. They did not have any effect on Anna though. She was still very angry. And when Armando realized this, he knew he'd just have to wait.

"It was a trip seeing him," he said, quietly.

"Do you look like him?" she asked, barely avoiding eye contact.

Armando nodded.

"How long did you talk to him for?"

"Not long. I spent most of the time screaming at him. He said that he was sick with cancer and that he was gonna die soon. I lost it after that."

"He came up to see you because he was dying?"

"Yeah."

Armando pulled Anna close and she allowed it. While they hugged, Armando squeezed her in all the places only he knew about. Her favorite places to be squeezed. Anna was the one who ended the hug this time when it was usually the other way around.

"I really messed it up with us. I'm sorry."

Anna didn't say anything. Her eyes responded by welling up.

"There's nothing I can do?"

"You can do things," she said, shaking her head slowly. "But I don't know if you will. And the scary part is, I'm not sure if I'm willing to wait for you anymore."

"I couldn't sleep last night. Most of it was because of us. But some of it—I don't know how much—was because of him."

"I'm not your girlfriend, so you don't *have* to listen to my opinion."

"But I know you have one," Armando said, looked back at her sadly.

"Would you like my opinion?"

He nodded.

"I think you should see him again. And I think you should invite him to watch you do the thing that you love most."

Armando wiped his eyes.

"The first game is Friday, right?"

He nodded.

"There you go."

The faint sound of the bell came from school.

Anna turned and started to walk away from Armando.

"Anna."

She turned around. Armando walked over to her. He took her hand and bent down to nuzzle his face close to hers. His lips brushed her cheek. She always loved that.

"Please," he whispered.

"No," she said. "I'm done."

They looked at each other right in the eyes.

Anna leaned in to kiss him softly on the mouth. The kiss was so perfect and all-consuming that it took Armando a few moments to realize that the kiss had actually ended.

14

ARMANDO COULDN'T SLEEP THE NIGHT BEFORE THE first game of the season. His insomnia hadn't stemmed from pregame jitters, rather all of the other mess swirling around him. Before leaving the house for school, he made sure to give his mother a kiss on the forehead as she slept heavily after a another double shift at the hospital. He left the house and went to Abuela's. He knocked on the door and waited for an answer. When his *abuela* answered instead of Oswaldo, relief flooded his veins. He wasn't sure why he was doing what he was doing. Maybe it was based on Anna's recommendation or maybe not. Whatever the impetus, it felt right.

"*Mijo,*" she said. "What are you doing here this early?"

"*Hola, Abuela,*" he said. "I was just wondering if Oswaldo is staying here with you?"

"You mean your father?"

"Yes."

"He is staying here with me but he's not in now. He went out. He said he wanted to walk around town."

"Okay."

"Should I tell him that you came looking for him?"

Armando thought for a moment. "Actually, do you know where he's walking? I can find him and pick him up."

"He said he was going to walk around the neighborhood where the three of you lived before . . . "

Armando kissed his grandmother on the forehead.

"I love you," he said.

"*Te amo, mijo.*"

"Bye, Grandma."

"Oh and *mijo*. No more stories. Go and find out for yourself."

Armando nodded and ran to his car.

Memories of his old neighborhood were faint in his mind. He and his mother had moved away from it right after his father left. He took a couple of turns, and the street names started to resonate. Soon, he was staring at his father's back. Oswaldo was standing in front of a decaying, one-story house.

* *

"Get in," Armando called out to his father.

Oswaldo stomped out the cigarette and walked over to the passenger side of Armando's car. Armando leaned over and opened the door. Oswaldo slid into the seat.

"With the diagnosis you have, you should really give those up. In case you haven't heard, they are the leading cause of cancer."

Oswaldo didn't respond to that. He was just happy to be near his son.

"I'm not here to give you a second chance or to ask you a bunch of questions about the past. I just wanted to tell you that you are welcome to come to my football game tonight. It's the first game of the season. I'll leave you a ticket at the box office if you want to come."

"I'll be there."

"But I want you to know. That *this* is it. This is all you're gonna get from me. You can come watch me play. Once. And that's all."

"*Si,*" Oswaldo said with a soothing nod. "Thank you, *mijo.*"

"Do you need a ride somewhere?"

"No. I'm just gonna be around here a little while longer. And then I'll walk to your *abuela*'s."

"What is this place?" Armando asked, nodding to the old house.

"This," he said, before a violent set of coughs

slashed his throat. "This is the house your mother had you in. It feels like it all just happened yesterday."

Oswaldo wheezed and his chest burned.

Armando tried his best to not let it get to him. But it was hard. He wanted to weep and maybe, weep in his father's arms. Something inside stopped him though. He couldn't afford to get close and then have the old man die on him. It had to be this way.

"Tonight then," Armando said looking away from his father.

Oswaldo nodded again. "Okay, son. Tonight. I'll be there."

Armando waited for his father to get out of the car and walk back over to the old house before pulling away. After all these years, he didn't want to know why his father left him and his mother. He didn't want to know what his father was doing in Mexico. Those answers did not matter to him. Sure, he had ideas. Some of the kids in the neighborhood had mentioned that their fathers knew of Oswaldo, and that he was into some bad stuff in Mexico. Armando wasn't sure if he believed it—and at this point, did not care about the truth.

Similarly, Armando did not want to answer a bunch of his father's questions about himself, his girlfriend, his football life. Armando thought that his greatest response would be made on the field later that evening. His father could see what he had been missing all of those years, and maybe the old man could die with a little pride in his chest, for his son, Armando, was a big, American football star.

. . . .

El Dorado's stands were packed for the first game of the season against crosstown rival Eastlake High School. There was a buzz in the air, not only for the new season, but also due to the lofty expectations surrounding El Dorado's team.

Armando was at peace before the game. He knew his mother was in the stands, along with his uncle Gus and cousin Raul. Those were the people he loved. He also felt good about leaving the ticket at the box office for his father. He was sad about Anna, but he treated the hole in his heart much like he did a nagging injury. He put it out of his mind. Forgetting about Anna would not be easy, but football at least provided the escape he needed.

The switch to left tackle had gotten smoother, with each practice leading up to the first game. He made fewer mental mistakes and always remembered to fire off the ball now. The occasional flub happened when he confused a call or forgot an audible; those things could be ironed out in time.

Right before the kickoff, Clark came over to Armando and stood next to him on the sideline.

"I know it's not how you planned it," Clark said. "But you're still a big part of this team. Maybe the biggest."

"I got you, Coach," Armando said.

Armando smiled. "But like I said before, next season, make sure you have a left tackle."

"I'll make sure."

Eastlake kicked off to El Dorado, and the home team ran it out to its own forty-yard line.

"Let's go offense!" Clark yelled.

Armando ran onto the field with the rest of the first stringers. The players formed a huddle around Freddie. He called the first official play of the season. It was a simple, off-tackle power play to Armando's side. When he reached the line of scrimmage, Armando realized that Eastlake had a huge defensive line. Each defender was heavier than that of El Dorado's defensive lineman—the ones Armando was used to going up against in practice. He was thankful for all those lower-body days in the weight room with Mad Dog during the summer.

Freddie snapped the ball, and Armando fired off the line and blocked down on the defensive tackle. After teaming up with his left guard, Armando climbed the ladder to the second level of the defense to search for a linebacker. He ended up getting a good piece of Eastlake's middle linebacker, and because of his block, Howard Martino ran for a sixty-yard touchdown. The season was only thirty seconds old, and El Dorado was up seven to nothing, due in large part to Armando.

Offit was the first one to congratulate Armando as he came off the field after the extra point.

"Combo block, Salguera!" he said. "Woo! Combo block! You just learned it on Tuesday!"

Clark was there too. He patted Armando on the helmet. "Good job."

"Thanks Coach."

After Eastlake's three and out, El Dorado took possession of the ball once again in good field position. The first play of the drive was another Martino run, off-tackle to the right, away from Armando. The play gained twenty-four yards. Although the run went away from Armando, he did a nice job of cutting off the backside defensive end. The second play was a sweep to the left, which allowed him to show off his athleticism by pulling out in front and leading the way for Martino. Behind Armando's crushing block of a poor and unfortunate cornerback, Martino was able to run untouched to Eastlake's three-yard line.

Clark called another off-tackle run behind Armando on the next play. When Eastlake's defensive coaches signaled for its goal line personnel, two extra defensive linemen trotted onto the field. The defense had an extra lineman right across from Armando with the hope of clogging the running game with the beefed up front. On the snap, Armando attacked the defender right in front of him and rooted the player out of the hole. Armando kept his legs churning and was able to cave in the entire right side of the defensive line. The resulting hole was vast enough that Martino *walked* in for his second touchdown. Just like that, El Dorado was up fourteen to nothing.

El Dorado's sideline went crazy. As Armando ran toward the frenzy, he realized that he would get no recognition or accolades for his team's success that season. Catches and touchdowns—those were his tangible imprints of the game before that night. He had to get used to the life of an offensive lineman—at least for the season.

Offit came over and grabbed Armando's helmet with both hands. He spat a wad of tobacco onto the turf before looking Armando in his eyes.

"I know I was hard on you those first couple of practices, but it's only because I knew you could take it."

"It's okay."

"Both of the touchdowns were made possible by *you*," he said. "Don't forget that."

Armando nodded.

Offit tapped the back of Armando's helmet before walking over to Clark.

Armando looked into the stands as El Dorado fans went crazy. Somewhere up there his father was proud. He wasn't sure why he thought of Oswaldo first, ahead of his mother, uncle and cousin. But he did, and decided to let all of the questions go for once.

El Dorado won the game forty-two to seven on the strength of five rushing touchdowns. Freddie only threw five passes the entire game. Without Armando in there at tight end, this was the formula that Mike had envisioned for the season. In addition to those first two touchdowns, Armando opened the holes for two more rushing touchdowns in the third quarter. He didn't play in the fourth quarter because the backups were in. As a whole, he rated his first game as an offensive lineman a complete success. There was no time to rest on that success as there would be tougher opponents to play that season. Armando knew there was still a lot to learn about his new position.

. . . .

Armando knew his father was in the stands that night because he checked with the box office after the game. He kept his promise and did not see Oswaldo Durante ever again. About three weeks later, Abuela stopped by his house to tell him that his father had died quietly and peacefully in her home. Armando didn't cry when Abuela told him the news; he simply held her while she did.

As for Anna, she kept her word and never got back together with Armando, despite several spirited attempts by him. They remained close friends during the next year and half of high school after the breakup and even slept together a number of times. But each time Armando insisted that they get back together and even marry, Anna rebuffed him and spouted some variation of a phrase about "their dreams not aligning."

Anna ended up accepting a scholarship to Dartmouth, and after leaving El Paso for New Hampshire, she and Armando spoke from time to time over the phone during the first couple of years of college until the phone calls stopped happening somewhere early in their junior years.

Armando went back to playing tight end during his senior year at El Dorado and lit up the state record books on the way to leading the team to the District One–Six A Playoffs. He earned a full athletic scholarship to the University of Southern California—as a tight end—and was eventually drafted in the third round by the Kansas City Chiefs, the same team that drafted Tony Gonzalez. During his first few seasons with the Chiefs, Armando saw spot duty on offense, and it wasn't until his fourth season that he exploded for nine receiving touchdowns and a spot on the AFC Pro Bowl team. With his dream realized and firmly in hand, he married a woman whom he had met in college, and shortly after the wedding, they had their first child—a baby boy. The child's name was Armando Durante Salguera II. Armando did not use his father's last name as his son's middle name out of any kind of love for or acceptance of his father. He did it to make Abuela happy.